The Heart of the Spring

Laura L. Valenti

Ann and Sam,
God bless you
wherever He leads!
Laura L. Valenti
1st Corinthians 13

INFINITY
PUBLISHING

ISBN 0-7414-6000-9

Printed in the United States of America

Cover photographs include historical material of the Bennett Spring area, courtesy of the state of Missouri Department of Natural Resources.

Cover artwork design is by Eric Adams of Lebanon, Missouri.

Published October 2010

INFINITY PUBLISHING
1094 New DeHaven Street, Suite 100
West Conshohocken, PA 19428-2713
Toll-free (877) BUY BOOK
Local Phone (610) 941-9999
Fax (610) 941-9959
Info@buybooksontheweb.com
www.buybooksontheweb.com

Dedication

Dedicated to each and every one who has ever come into the valley of Brice and Bennett and the Osages' Sacred One and fallen in love, with a place, with a spirit, with the heart of Bennett Spring.

And with gratitude to God for the gift of this beautiful place, that many of us may visit and some have come to call their own sweet home.

Author's Preface

On a cold winter's afternoon at Bennett Spring in early 2010, two friends who've worked in and loved the area for years told me, "We need a book, something that tells the story of Bennett Spring for visitors who come here. You're a writer. Can't you do something about that?"

At the time I laughed and told them it must be a slow day at work. After a short visit, I continued on my way which included a brisk afternoon walk in the frigid sunshine along the spring branch. Even so, their suggestion kindled a spark and within less than a day it was a bonfire, a complete story burning a hole in my soul, waiting to be told. I've never written a novel so quickly, the words flying from my fingers to the computer keyboard to the screen. I truly believe this isn't my story, but rather one given to me by the good Lord and it is simply my privilege and honor to put it down on paper. For that I am most grateful!

To me, history has always been like a wondrous storybook, just waiting to be shared. For as long as I can remember, my favorite books and movies are the ones that end with a brief paragraph saying the hero, civil rights leader, sports legend, or the mother or dad who lived down the block, went on to do this or that and now lives in London, New York or rural Montana with their spouse and children.

Historical fiction works in much the same way, a set of made-up characters who lived, worked and struggled through the times of a historical event with which we are often quite familiar. A few of the persons named in this book, Josephine Bennett Smith, William Sherman Bennett, William Lenz, Rev. Louie Bennett, Rev. George Bolds, Uncle Jim Clanton and Arlie Bramwell were real people who lived or worked in the Bennett Spring area at the time the Missouri state government was looking for a place to establish its first state park. Lee Taylor, along with his brothers, John and Thomas Taylor, operated Taylor Brothers Manufacturing in St. Louis, making butter churns in conjunction with others, and many antique dealers throughout the country are familiar with their legacy. They were my father's uncles. Likewise, locations like the Brice Inn, the Bennett Store, the grist mill and trout hatchery at Bennett Spring were real places in 1924.

All the other persons in this book are completely fictional as are all of the conversations and daily events. All of what transpires here is intended strictly for the purpose of entertainment and to shed a little light on what life might have been like for those who lived in the Bennett Spring area before there was a state park. It is not a historical account, but rather a story that provides another way to learn about the historical framework in which important events took place, events that still affect our way of life decades later.

Like many others who now claim Bennett Spring as home, I came to this valley over 30 years ago, a transplant as a result of my husband's career with the Missouri Department of Conservation. Warren worked over 20 years as the assistant manager of the trout hatchery during the 1980s and 1990s. As a result of that job, we were blessed to live in state housing in the park our first eight years here and then moved to our own home a couple of miles up the road. We raised four children at Bennett Spring and I know wherever they go in this world, like me, they will always think of Bennett Spring fondly, with great memories.

I sincerely hope that this book will be received in the same spirit it was written, as an offering from someone who has long loved Bennett Spring and the folks who call it home, whether for a few years or a lifetime.

My sincere thanks to those who have assisted with this manuscript and helped me to better appreciate the history of the area over the years, including Ellen Gray Massey, well known Ozark author and editor, for her tireless editing, encouragement and wise counsel; Eric Adams, Laclede County's own photographic wizard for a beautiful cover and his enthusiasm for this project; Jim and Carmen Rogers for generous material support; Diane Tucker for her support and willingness to share history and photos; my father, Rogers H. Taylor of San Diego and my uncle, Ronnie Taylor of Thayer Missouri, for sharing stories of their uncles' business; Mary Lambert and fellow novelist D.B. Barratt for their knowledge and belief in the spirit of writing; my husband, Warren, for his patience with my passion for writing and for bringing me to Bennett Spring in the first place; and last but certainly not least, my thanks to Sue Eckmann of the Bennett Spring Park Store and Diane Tucker, Bennett Spring Park Naturalist, for the original inspiration to write a story about this, our favorite place, Bennett Spring. My prayer is that you will enjoy reading it as much as I've enjoyed writing it!

Laura L. Valenti, author
Bennett Spring, Missouri

Chapter 1

"He can't do it, I'm telling you! I don't know how to stop him but we got to find a way!" Zeb Darling burst into the cozy kitchen of his home above what was known far and wide as Bennett Spring and threw his weathered leather mail carrier onto the table in disgust.

His daughter Becky looked up in alarm from where she was stuffing an extra piece of kindling into the wood cook stove. The black cat that had been sitting on the window ledge scurried for cover in the far corner of the room. Becky dropped the heavy iron lid back into place and picked up the tall blue-steel coffee pot, pouring her father his customary cup as he came in from making his rounds. As the mail carrier for the valley, Zeb Darling delivered mail to folks up and down the spring banks each day before he headed out to the hills surrounding their valley.

"Pa, what is it?" Becky asked in surprise at her father's outburst. She slid two warm biscuits onto a chipped china plate alongside a sizzling slice of ham and set it on the table beside the hot cup of coffee in front of the fuming man. Flanked by a pat of fresh-churned butter and a small jar of honey, the enticing aromas went unnoticed as he gestured with the knife he was using to butter the biscuits.

"Those Bennetts. They're going to sell us all out to the state government for a park. Can you imagine that?!"

"Oh." Becky's long blond hair fell across her face, hiding her expression as she turned away, but not quickly enough.

"Oh? Oh? Is that all you can say? What do you know about this, girl? You're right down there in the thick of it every day at that hotel, and you've not said a word about it."

"Well, I, uh…." She stammered, not wanting to add to her father's angst. She threw a quick glance towards her mother who was busy at the rug loom in the far corner of the room.

Without speaking, Hannah Darling continued to sling the shuttle and slam the strips tightly together as the parts of the large loom shifted in unison, keeping her hands and feet moving at all times.

"I didn't say anything before, Pa." Becky quickly realized she was on her own in this conversation and opted for the truth as the path of least resistance. "Mostly because, well, Miz Josie, she said it was a secret. Secret negotiations, that's what she called it. And she told me not to say nothing to nobody so…"

"So-o-o." Her father heaved a weary sigh. "That means you came home and told your mama and not another living soul! I mean, William Sherman Bennett runs the store and the post office is in the store, but he is being totally hush-mouthed about this whole thing. You know more than you're telling!"

"Pa, I…I," she hesitated, glancing towards the corner once more before letting her eyes fall to her eleven-year-old brother, Benji, who continued to play quietly with a handful of tin soldiers on the floor near his mother's feet.

"Go ahead. Call me a liar, girl. I'm a-waiting." The corners of his mouth twitched even as he tried to maintain his stern tone, arms folded across his chest.

"Oh, Pa." Becky grinned, realizing her father's frustration had less to do with her and more to do with the situation. "You know me too well."

"Don't you know what this means to all of us? I appreciate Miz Josie wanting to keep this quiet. That works to her advantage, I'm sure, but for the rest of us, it's nothing short of a disaster!" He stopped speaking long enough to stuff half of a biscuit, dripping with honey, into his mouth. He casually brushed both edges of his drooping sandy mustache, dusting away crumbs, both real and imagined.

Becky turned back from the stove and looked directly at her father. At age eighteen, she'd been out of school for some time now and working at Josephine Bennett Smith's Brice Inn this year, she had learned so much. She adored her father, despite his gruff ways and overly direct manner. Still sometimes, it seemed to her, he understood so little of the world.

"Pa," she began as gently as she knew how, "this is true progress for this valley. Tourists and other townspeople are already coming out here, more all the time. A park will mean more people and more money for everyone. Don't you see that?"

"No, I can't say as I see that at all. I see it will mean more for the Bennetts, there's no doubt of that, but do you not understand that the land they aim to sell is what the whole town of Brice sits on? Now how does that benefit anyone but them? The truth is they're going to sell our town right out from under us and that means the post office, too, Missy. Once that's gone, what do you think this family is going to do for money? Don't get me wrong. We're doing fine, what with my job, and your mama's help, here and there, and now even you working some but if I lose this postal route, that's going to be a mighty blow. And no town means no post office. You best be thinking about that while you're supporting your friends in the hotel business!" He cast a strange and mournful look in her mother's direction that Becky couldn't read.

"Oh, Pa, I don't believe it. They can't sell a whole town!" She hesitated for a moment. "Can they?"

"You mark my words, Miss Priss." He went back to cutting the air with his butter knife as he spoke. "This is something we better figure out a way to put a stop to or...or..." He left the threat unfinished and busied himself with buttering the second biscuit.

"Ma, can they really do that?" Becky slipped off her apron and hung it on a peg behind the door. She cast a critical eye over her clothes, using her hands to press imaginary wrinkles from her long skirt, the hem of which dusted the tops of her lace up shoes.

"Hmm," was her mother's only immediate response.

"I'm telling you, Hannah." Her husband began again.

"Sounds to me like Sherman Bennett isn't the only one leading with his pocketbook." The woman of the house finally spoke.

"Now what is that supposed to mean?" Her husband's exasperation turned in a new direction.

"But lay up for yourselves, treasure in heaven...For where your treasure is, there will your heart be also."

"There she goes, quoting scripture." He shook his head. "I declare sometimes your mama speaks in parables more than Jesus himself!"

"Being compared to my Lord is no small compliment, sir," she commented without looking up as she continued to weave.

"Now am I to take it that you're telling me I'm no different than—"

"You heard me," was her only response.

"Pa, what's a park?" Benji spoke up from the rug where he had been lying. "What's it for?"

"What indeed?" His father snorted as he stood up. "Got to go, girls. And you, too, son." He grinned in spite of his dark mood. "No matter what else goes on the mail must be delivered and as a sworn employee of the U.S. Post Office that means it's up to me!" He glanced over at Benji. "What's a park, heh? Let's see…something that can cause a lot of trouble to a whole lot of people, if you ask me. Now come on, up with you. Get your jacket. Betsy and I will leave you off at school on our way."

He heaved his mail sack onto his shoulder and kissed his wife on the forehead while she remained seated at the loom. He moved carefully despite his load.

"Watch out, Shakespeare," he muttered, moving the cat from beneath his feet, with a gentle shove. With a quick wave to Becky, he swept out the door and swung himself up into the saddle. Once seated on Betsy, his sure-footed buckskin mustang, he reached down and pulled his son up behind him. Benji grinned at Becky, who stood framed in the doorway as they headed down the trail towards the spring.

Betsy was a good example of her father's old-fashioned ways, Becky thought a moment later, as she stood on the porch and looked down at the fresh balls of manure that Betsy had left on the ground before her. It was 1924 after all and other mail carriers in the area had bought motorized vehicles in recent years. Zebulon Darling insisted, however that the poor excuses for roads along his postal route were still too rough, plagued by mud holes, tire-puncturing sharp rocks and other hazards that made those expensive and not-always-so-dependable automobiles impractical for an Ozarks mailman.

"You be a good boy today and keep Ma company, Homer." Becky reached down and patted the head of the speckled blue tick hound at her side. She scratched his ears as he rolled his head side to side to enjoy every bit of the attention. She tied her sunbonnet in place and stepped off the porch.

Like her father, she was on her way to a job, which made her feel incredibly grown up, working for Miz Josie at the Brice Inn on a daily basis. She set a brisk pace for herself in the cool crisp air as she approached the spring in all its misty gray-green beauty on a bright spring morning. As always, the icy cold waters looked as if they were boiling to the surface placidly, silently rolling, coming up from their birthplace somewhere deep in the heart of the earth. The spring provided water, a basic of life, for area residents but also, increasingly, it was a natural attraction for visitors coming from far and near, a place to relax and refresh the body and the spirit.

The return of spring meant the hills were dotted with the white flowers of the dogwood, bursting forth in all their glory, practically trumpeting the arrival of the new season. The sun sprinkled through the budding trees and the riotous greenery sparkling bright at every step was still spattered with the last of the tiny bright pink blossoms of the redbud trees. Freed from their long winter's nap, peeper and now tree frogs sang at the top of their lungs all day and much of the night, calling to one another to begin anew the cycle of life.

She was pleased to see the water was well within its usual banks, allowing her to make her way easily down the spring trail that ran along the west side of the stream for a little over a half mile. She stepped cautiously along the narrow trek, strewn as it was with rocks, roots, nooks and crannies of all description.

The sleek, tiny brown mink that lived under a bank overhang just a few hundred feet below the spring dove into his hidey hole at her approach. Becky quickened her step in time to see him turn and hiss at her before disappearing from sight. His indignation always made her laugh as if they didn't meet this way at least once or twice a week. She continued on her way, keeping a vigilant eye on the water, catching glimpses of the fish that glided by.

Suckers, bass, sunfish and the much-discussed trout, stocked by both private and public concerns on occasion, slipped through the frigid sun-dappled shallows. Fishing, whether it was gigging suckers or catching any and all with a cane pole, was a favorite pastime of many an area resident and Becky was no exception. She glanced longingly at the water once more, thinking about the delectable delicacies that swam in there, as she reached the new trout hatchery.

The flange bridge that ran just below the crib dam next to the newly-constructed trout hatchery was designed for motorized automobiles.

She stopped to watch a Model T negotiate the bridge's steel rails with the large square holes running down the center. She had taken a dare more than once from her brothers to slip across the rails of the flange bridge, even though it was definitely not designed for foot traffic. She tried not to think of the scolding she'd be catching one day soon when her mother heard about such stunts.

The water roared over the crib dam behind her, the water resounding as it rushed over the cribs, big timber boxes that had been strung together to create the natural wood barrier. It was a comforting sound she had been accustomed to all of her life, the power of the water rushing over the dam. No matter the structures that men had built in this valley along and across the water—mills, bridges, and dams—sooner or later, the power of the water always won.

She hurried on, climbing over the rough rail fence rather than going on down to the nearest gate. The fence surrounded the hotel, nearby store and the few other town buildings, keeping the free range stock--wandering cattle, horses, sheep and a few goats--at bay.

"Morning, Miz Josie," she called out as she opened the front door of the two-story white clapboard Brice Inn, taking an extra second or two to wipe her damp feet on the mat outside.

She slipped behind the front desk and checked the registration book first. No one else had come in since she left the night before, but she always liked to check, just the same. One guest, Mr. Eugene Fredericks, the traveling salesman who stopped here about once a month, had left early this morning so that meant she had one room to clean. There were two other rooms rented out right now. Room number one was occupied by Mr. and Mrs. Jones, visiting their son and his wife and their seven children who lived further up the valley. Becky had overheard Mrs. Jones telling Josie when they checked in that she realized it was customary for relatives to stay with local family members when possible. She was, however, the new Mrs. Jones, recently married to the widower Jones from up near Rolla, and the idea of staying with a houseful of children she'd only just met was not particularly appealing. Her new husband had been kind enough to suggest they spend their four days here rather than at her new in-laws' home, a decision she said that made her love him all the more. Becky thought that was particularly sweet.

The other room was rented to an older single man, Mr. George Thompson, who had arrived two days ago with a large camera and other photographic equipment. He said he hoped to catch up with William Lenz, a local photographer who had taken and published many well known photographs of Bennett Spring in the past. It sounded like Mr. Thompson might be around for awhile.

She pulled the heavy turkey feather duster out of the closet tucked under the steps and made a quick round of the entry and parlor area, dusting off the wooden end tables, the buffet table, chest of drawers and other wooden-trimmed furniture in the room.

"Well, good morning. Miss Becky," Josie greeted her as she came out of the kitchen. She often called her Miss Becky, as if she was a woman full grown, a fact that further endeared Miz Josie to her heart.

"Morning, Ma'am," Becky answered. "I guess you didn't hear me when I first came in a little bit ago. I hollered but I wasn't sure where you were."

"Oh, I was back there, chopping onions, taters and carrots, making stew for dinner today," Josie said, as she swept a stray lock of dark hair from her forehead. "Not sure how many we'll have at noon, but it's looking like it'll be a fine day so who knows? That photographer might be around and some of the fellers from the saw mill will stop in if we got something that appeals to 'em so thought I might as well use up the last of the vegetables from the root cellar. And with it being stew, if'n they don't eat it today, it'll be good for days yet to come, don't you know." She winked at Becky and giggled like a school girl less than half her age.

"Yes, Ma'am." Becky grinned as she bent over to roll up the wool runner that led from the front door to the front desk. It was one of her mother's best creations, she thought, as she took it outside to throw over the clothesline in the back and beat the dust out of it.

After the rugs, it was off to the kitchen to wash the breakfast dishes and any pots and pans used in lunch preparations and then up to change the bed and straighten up Mr. Fredericks' now vacated room. The aroma of Miz Josie's beef and vegetable stew soon permeated the entire building, reminding Becky that it had been a long time since her own breakfast at home half a dozen hours ago. She had, of course, been up for a couple of hours by the time her father stopped on his mail route today. She'd milked their two cows before baking the biscuits and frying the sliced ham. It always seemed like time absolutely flew here working for Miz Josie and now, as she tucked in the fresh sheets on the bed she had just changed, it was time to go wait tables in the parlor for those who came for a noon day hot meal at the inn.

"Hey, Becky," Red Flaherty, a regular diner and a top hand at the grist mill, called out from his seat in the dining room as she walked in. "What's good today?"

"Miz Josie's got beef stew, cornbread, and lemme see…" She ducked into the kitchen and came back immediately. "Apple cobbler for dessert."

"Hmm." Red closed his eyes and licked his lips in anticipation. "Sounds like a meal fit for a king to me! Send it on out. I'll be right back. Couple of the boys are over to the Bennett Store and they said they wanted to know what was for dinner today. I told 'em I'd come find out and let 'em know. Might have a couple more customers for you in a few minutes."

"That'd be fine." Becky smiled, knowing some of the workers at both the saw mill and at Bennett's best known grist mill were too shy to ask about the daily midday fare. Red, on the other hand, wasn't afraid to ask anybody anything, Becky thought. She sighed as she watched him walk out the door, and thought fleetingly of her older brother, Jacob, wishing he was still working at one of the nearby mills like Red. She turned from the window and busied herself with making certain she had everything lined out that she would need for noon time diners.

True to his word, Red brought in a couple more fellows and soon Becky was too busy filling plates with food, glasses with spring water and cups with hot coffee, to worry about anything else.

After everyone else was served and satisfied, Becky filled a plate for herself and joined Josie at her own table, situated close by the full length curtain that separated the parlor from the kitchen.

"Hey, Josie," Red Flaherty called out from the table closest to the front door. "What's all this about a park anyway? We're hearing all kinds of stories over at the grist mill. You going to sell this place to the state so they can make a right nice little park out of it all? How's them boys up river going to get their wheat ground regular if this turns into some kind of Yellowstone Place?"

"Now boys." Josie adopted her best conciliatory tone that Becky had heard her use to settle more than one argument, from politics to religion and all topics in between. "Don't you know better than to listen to all that mill yammering? Ain't nobody got nothing better to do over there when they're waiting for their grain than to flap their gums and make up 'bout anything that comes into their heads?" She laughed softly. "You think the state is really going to pay hard cash money for that sort of thing?"

Red shrugged and stuck out his lower lip, realizing he wasn't going to get any real information from the lady of the house. His companions laughed and nodded, in a teasing manner, seeming to agree with Josie's logic.

"Well, you never know 'til you ask," Red answered back with a grin.

"That's true." Josie smiled and raised a glass of cold tea in his direction.

"But supposin' just for a minute, it was true." Red wasn't ready to let the subject die a natural death. "What do you think? Would you throw in with 'em?"

"Well, now, Red." Josie leaned back as if seriously contemplating his question for the very first time. "Just about everything ever wrought by man on God's green earth is for sale one way or 'tother, so I guess it would all depend on the price they were offering, wouldn't it? A park wouldn't be such a bad idea when you think about it. Something to keep the spring and the fishing all set aside for people to enjoy like they do here and now but forever. They could make a real go of that fish hatchery over there and have lots of trout all year round. Bring in more tourists, of course, too, and keep the big loggers from clear-cutting every hillside around. Who knows?" She shrugged with her most disarming grin. "It might be a right good idea."

"The truth is, you've got fewer people coming to use the grist mill every year." A voice from the other side of the room spoke up. Bespectacled George Thompson, the photographer, had been the last one to come in and the last one Becky had served a full noonday meal before sitting down to her own dinner. "A great many people are taking their grain into the bigger town mills and others are buying their flour and corn meal at the mercantile in sacks already ground. I don't mean to state the painful or the obvious, gentlemen, but the magazine I'm working for right now asked for photos of several different mills, because their business is dwindling as things change."

"You're right about one thing," Red spoke back sharply to the newcomer. "It's not the news anyone around here wants to hear."

Mr. Thompson shrugged and returned to silence, but Becky thought about what he had said and realized how true it was. When she was younger, even just a few years ago, she remembered the wagons used to line up at harvest time, with farmers and their families spending days in line sometimes, to get their wheat ground. Miz Josie had commented to her privately more than once how much more she preferred tourists to farmers. Tourists came on vacation and spent their money freely as opposed to the farmers, who might rent one room where the whole family could wash up and half would sleep, and they guarded their every expenditure closely. In recent years, the farmers came in smaller numbers with each passing season. She hadn't really considered the why of it all before. The truth is until this last year she'd paid little attention as the adults discussed such things long and sometimes loudly over their meals at the Brice Inn, as they met and shopped at the Bennetts' store or around their own dinner tables at home.

"Whether a person wants to hear it or not," Josie defended all her guests equally. "That doesn't make it any less a fact, Red Flaherty, and facts are, even in a little backwater place like Brice, the world keeps a-changing. You got two choices, the way I see it, change with it or become a dinosaur."

"A dinosaur?"

"Yes, a dinosaur. You know, one of those big lizards that lived centuries ago—"

"I know what a dinosaur is, Josie, but I—"

"If you don't change with the times, Red, you become a dinosaur and then you are extinct!"

At that, his dinner companions burst into laughter as they all got to their feet to return to work. "A dinosaur. Is that you, Red?" one asked.

"Did they have any red-headed dinosaurs a-way back then? Have to look in them books in the library in Lebanon and see," guffawed another, with a good-natured clap on Red's shoulder.

They trooped out the door as Josie stood by and collected their money with a sweet smile. "It's all good, Red," she told him, the last one to pay. "We'll still be cooking for you tomorrow. Of that, I'm certain."

"Well, these days, it's good to be certain of something anyway," he added with a lopsided smile.

"Red," Josie spoke to him once more as he stood in the doorway. "How's your mama doing?"

Red sighed as he pulled his cap from where he'd stuffed it into the back pocket of his overalls. "She's not good, that's for sure. None of them doctors in Springfield seem to be able to help her. She gets thinner every day, I swear, just sort of wasting away, no matter what we do."

"I'm sorry to hear it." Josie's voice lost all its teasing familiarity from a few moments before. "Give her my best, will you? And when you get off work today, you stop by here and take her a piece of that apple cobbler, ya hear?"

"I'll do it, Josie. Thank you." His voice caught as he hurried out onto the front porch.

George Thompson shook his head slightly as he signed a ticket for his dinner and headed upstairs to his room.

"Miz Josie." Becky waited dutifully until they were back sitting at their table, finishing the last of their meal. "I thought you said all this park business was in secret," she half-whispered, casting a furtive glance over her shoulder at the now empty dining room. "My pa was talking about it this morning and now Red Flaherty…"

"Like anything else in this valley that starts out a secret," Josie sniffed in disdain, "it don't stay that way long. No matter really." She sighed heavily. "My brother is discussing all the business of it with this one and that. I have no idea how it will all come out in the end. We'll just have to wait and see." She leaned back in her chair, a weariness resting upon her that was not apparent just a few moments ago when she was bantering with Red Flaherty.

Next to her own mother, Miz Josie Bennett Smith was the woman that Becky admired most in the world. She seemed so much more worldly than others she had encountered in her life here in the valley, and unlike so many, she never treated Becky like a child, but rather like a woman of equal stature. It was a compliment that was not lost on the teenager.

"Well, I think it's a wonderful idea. A park, I mean." Becky hurried on. "It's like you said, it would mean protection for the spring and the land hereabouts, but it would bring more people and that means more money for everyone. My pa says, though..." She hesitated, trying to think about how best to paraphrase her father's objections.

"Miz Josie." She decided to try a question instead. "What about the town? What will happen to Brice if this all becomes a park?"

"Ah, yes, Brice," Josie sighed again. "Not much here, really, Becky, my girl. Never has been and I don't see anything that says that's going to change. I'm afraid the town of Brice will become a victim of progress with the coming of a park, but that's probably going to happen regardless. It's simply a matter of time. You've heard of ghost towns before. It strikes me it wouldn't take a lot for Brice to become another. It's sad but it happens."

Becky had not considered that possibility until now and she stopped eating, leaving half of her apple cobbler still in the bowl in front of her. "But Miz Josie." She heaved a deep sigh. "Doesn't that just break your heart?"

"Oh, Becky. There have been lots of comings and goings in this life to break my heart, but no, I can't say the loss of Brice is one of them." She took a deep breath and reached across the table to pat the hand of her young friend. "It's nothing to fret about today. It may or may not happen but either way, I doubt that you or I are going to have a lot to say about the decidin' of it all. The men will decide and as is so often the case, we'll be left to pick up the pieces. The good news is we don't have to decide nothing today. There's dishes to do yet today and plans to be made for tomorrow. That's enough to keep us busy for now." And with that she was on her feet and headed for the kitchen, her own dishes in hand.

Becky managed to complete the rest of her work through the afternoon, but that didn't keep her mind off of all that she had heard throughout the day. She was still deep in thought walking home when she spotted the first kingfisher of the season, swooping low towards the water's surface, its hoarse cry echoing as it slipped through the air.

A rough running vehicle pulled up behind her. The driver squeezed the rubber bulb on the oversized horn hanging on the side of the door, causing her to jump.

"Whoa sister, whatcha doin'?" A rakishly handsome young man with bright blue eyes that matched her own leaned out the driver's window. "Wanna ride?"

"Jacob Abraham Darling!" she cried out in exasperation. "What are you doing in there?" A motorized car ride was still enough of a treat that Becky didn't wait for him to answer as she scooted around to the passenger door and climbed inside.

"Where have you been?" She punched him in the shoulder, almost knocking off the small battered cowboy hat he was wearing, as she peppered him with questions. "Whose automobile is this? Where are you going?"

"Slow down, kiddo." He laughed and pulled back onto the dirt road, with a grinding of gears. "I cain't answer that many questions at once."

"Oh, all right." She righted herself in the passenger seat next to her brother and peered expectantly out the front windshield. "Wow, what kind of auto is this anyway? Pretty fancy, huh?"

"Oh, ho, are we getting picky about what kind of ride we get these days?" he teased and she blushed as she giggled.

"It belongs to a friend, a 1915 Model T Touring car, or at least it was until it run off the road and turned over at the bottom of a ravine. When they rebuilt it, they made it into a sort of little truck. Pretty spiffy, don't you think?"

"Yes, it really is," she agreed as she looked it over, "but pretty noisy, or at least noisier than most."

"Oh, that's just from the turning over of it, I imagine," Jake added. "Doesn't seem to make any difference, just a little trickier to shift is all."

She tossed the heavy sweater that she'd needed earlier that morning behind her and then gasped as it disturbed a wool blanket that had been casually tossed over a variety of different items lying behind the driver's seat where the back seat had once been.

"Jacob, are you crazy? What are you doing with a hundred pound bag of sugar back there? Oh good heavens!" She jerked the blanket back further to reveal a coil of copper piping. "You got a worm in here too?! Pa was right. I heard him tell Ma he was afraid you was running with Buster Kendrix up there on Poker Ridge and it's true! You're up there makin'—"

He cut her off. "Now, Sis, don't go thinking the worst, when you don't know—"

"Don't go thinking?! That's you, not me! You expect me to believe you and Buster are baking cakes with all that sugar? Now I know why you ain't been coming home at night. Pa will surely skin you alive if he finds you driving an auto with—"

Her tirade was cut short by the shrill squeal of a siren coming up behind them. Becky spun in her seat in time to see a black vehicle with a gold star on its door pull alongside them. The driver motioned for Jake to pull to the side of the road.

"So help me, Jacob Darling!" Becky hissed at her brother as she pounded his right shoulder. "If I go to jail for moonshinin', Pa won't have to do nothing 'cause I'll kill you myself and tell God you died!"

Chapter 2

As the sheriff's deputy climbed out of his car, Becky quickly rearranged the wool blanket and tossed some scraps of wood onto it that she found at her feet, as if the vehicle had been used to haul firewood recently.

"Afternoon." The deputy tipped his wide-brimmed hat in their direction. "Well, Jake, this is a surprise—" He stopped speaking altogether as he bent down to get a glimpse of the passenger. "Why, Becky, as I live and breathe!"

"Hullo, Cletus." Becky cast her eyes down but not before she caught the meaningful widening of Jake's. They threatened to bore a hole right through her as he turned his back momentarily on the man at his window. "How have you been?"

"Well, Becky, to be honest…" His voice trailed off and then he found his courage once again. "Can I, uh, maybe I'll just come over there and talk to you for a minute." He started around the front of their vehicle and Jake took the opportunity to slide his foot across the rubber boot supporting the stick shift between them and stomp on her toes.

"Becky, it's so good to see you again. Since I've been working for the sheriff, I don't get out here to Bennett Spring as often as I'd like, and I just, well…I mean, I wanted, you know after seeing you the last time at the Valentine's Day social at the Baptist church in town, and how that all went and all…." Deputy Cletus Meyers sputtered to a stop.

Becky had a sudden vision of Cletus in a white shirt, abruptly turned to pink when he was pushed by one of his friends, causing him to stumble into the refreshment table. He had tried valiantly to catch the punch bowl before it hit the floor but the results had been less than successful.

Becky stepped up to his rescue. "It's good to see you, too, Cletus," she cooed much more kindly than she felt, ever mindful of Jake's watchful eye. "Shouldn't you be telling us why you stopped us just now though? My brother was giving me a ride home from my new job at the Brice Inn, don't you know, and well, I don't want to be too late getting home to help my mama with the chores."

"Oh, sure Becky, I understand." Cletus stood up straight. "Well, to be honest, I pulled you all over, that's how we say it at the sheriff's department, because this here car was wanted, or at least the ones driving this car was, after a chase day before yesterday with one of the moonshiners. I don't figure that would be you, Becky."

"No, Cletus, that wouldn't be me," Becky laughed softly. "Are you sure you got the right automobile?"

"Well, I don't know. They just told us to watch out for...." He began searching his pockets, shirt and pants, and pulling out small pieces of paper that had various scribbled notes on them. "Who does this car belong to, anyway, Jake?"

"Well," Jake gave a little yawn as if he was already bored with the whole conversation, "that kind of depends on who you ask. It did belong to Frank Kendrix up by Springfield, but he turned it over in a gulley and pretty much wrecked it. After that, his brother, Leonard, got holt of it and fixed it up and now you can see it's running again, pretty fine. You know, this area is getting to be quite the market for used cars. Frank's got him a nice little business going, hauling used ones up here from Springfield. Have you got you one yet, Cletus?" He didn't wait for an answer. "Anyway, I borried it today from his son, just to run a little ol' errand across the valley. I would never have let my little sister get in it if I'd a known it was being used for illegal stuff. You know that, Cletus." He looked so contrite that even Becky believed him momentarily.

"You borrowed this car from Buster Kendrix? Now, Jake you ought to know better than that!" Cletus wasn't buying all of what Jake was selling.

"Honest, Cletus," Jake began again. "You know my pa! That kind of goings on wouldn't set well with him at all and—"

"Oh, don't even start with me." Cletus gave up his futile pocket search. "I can't find the right note anyway. Look, I don't want to get neither one of you in no trouble but we can't have moonshiners running the countryside neither. You for sure just taking Becky home?"

"Just taking my sister home and then I'll take this here vehicle right back where I got it." Jake held up three fingers in a mock salute. "Scout's honor. How's that?"

Cletus frowned but relented. "I guess it'll have to do for now." He turned his attention back to the vehicle's passenger. "Sure good to see you again, Becky. You coming to church in town again anytime soon?"

"Oh, I don't rightly know, Cletus." Becky kept her eyes trained on her feet as she spoke. "You know, I only get there when I go in to stay at Georgia McCandles' house once in awhile and I'm working now. Most of the time I just go to our little church out here at Brice but maybe later this summer, when it's warmer."

"Well, just the same. I hope to see you sometime soon." He cleared his throat and turned his attention back to the driver. The timbre of his voice changed as he tried to sound authoritative. "Jake, you drive on now but be careful who you go a-borrowing a car from, you hear?"

"I hear you, Cletus and I thank you. I'll be sure and be more careful from now on." He hid his smirk in his shirt sleeve as he pulled away, struggling with the difficult gear shift while guiding the car back onto the narrow dirt road.

"Jake, I swear---"

"Don't say nothing. It ain't all my fault. After all, we got lucky that your boyfriend there is as dumb as a box of rocks." His pent up laughter burst out as he glanced over his shoulder one more time. Cletus was still standing outside his own car, watching them drive away.

"First of all, he ain't my boyfriend." Becky smacked her brother on the shoulder again. "Second of all, he ain't so dumb as he's just awful nice and kinda shy. How he ever ended up working for the sheriff is something I can't understand! You got lucky, that's for sure. Lucky he didn't look under this blanket and luckier still that I don't just, just, oh, I swear, I don't know what to do with you!" She turned away to hide the mix of emotions that threatened to end in tears.

After a few moments of staring out the window into the thick green tangle of woods that covered the hillside across the spring branch, she spoke again. "Ma's been awful quiet and kinda sad lately. I really think she misses you, and I know Pa does, although he would never say it."

"Well, Becky girl, we each got our own problems. There ain't no doubt about that." He pushed his hat back further on his head as he drove. "I'd be the first one to say, I'm sorry things ain't going well between me and Pa, but I got to do what I think is right for a change. It cain't always be his way, no matter what he thinks. I know that puts you and Ma and even Benji, that brat, in a bad way but it just cain't be helped right now. I'll do good, you'll see. I ain't going to work for one of these rubes around here for no 35 cents an hour. I can do better than that. I know I can, and then Pa won't have no cause to be on me all the time." He pulled the car to a stop a few feet short of the big spring. "I ain't going to go no further just now. If Pa's home, there's no point in upsetting him by getting in sight of the house and having him fuss at you about me, if you know what I mean?"

"Yes, I know exactly what you mean, but thanks for the ride, anyway. Be careful, Jake. You need to find some better friends. Somebody other than Buster Kendrix, that's for sure." With that parting shot she climbed out of the car, while looking at the spring. She turned back to wave good-bye but her brother was already pulling the car around to head back the way they'd come.

Walking the short distance that skirted the head of the spring, Becky's eyes strayed to the rolling aquamarine waters as she passed by the source of fascination that some said put out a hundred million gallons of water a day.

She couldn't get her mind around that kind of a number. She leaned against a sycamore tree close by the water's edge and stared at the constantly moving waters. Her mind was reeling, trying to pull together all that she'd heard and seen today. From cross words with her father to the talk of this new park and especially troubling, the run in with Jake, her heart yearned for the peacefulness she had so often found in the past, just standing here watching the waters roll and turn over endlessly, coming from so deep below. Her thoughts couldn't be quieted today and soon her feet were moving again, running towards her home, situated south and west, less than a quarter mile above the spring. Her troubled thoughts were centered on her mother who was so quiet, practically lethargic of late. She wasn't sure what was going on, but she intended to find out.

Sassy, that's how her father had described Hannah Andersen the first time he'd laid eyes on her over twenty years ago at an auction in Lebanon. He was traveling through on his way to Denver, but the dark-haired, doe-eyed beauty had captivated him so completely that he never made it any further down the road.

Sassy certainly did not describe the shadow of the woman who had recently taken the place of the mother Becky had adored all of her life. A faint vision of Mrs. Mabel Flaherty, wasted and shaking the last time Becky had seen her, crept unbidden into her thoughts. Fear gripped her heart. Could some similar illness have taken hold of her mother as well? She said a silent prayer as she hurried on down the trail to her home. A striped chipmunk started at her approach and scampered up the trail before her, diving into its hole just ahead of her hurried footsteps.

Inside the house, Hannah Darling was still at the loom but the rug she had been working on all day was considerably longer than when Becky had left earlier that morning.

"Oh, it's beautiful, Ma." Becky ran her hands over the lumpy colorful surface. "Miz Josie will just love it. She wants one for each room, to put beside the bed. She says that way when her guests first get up in the morning, their feet will be on a nice warm rug and not the cold floor."

"Well, I hope she likes the ones I've made so far," her mother sighed and straightened her back to stretch. "Oh, Becky. I feel so, so…" She stood up and moved quickly out the door past her daughter, scurrying down the path that led to the outhouse in the back.

In a few moments, she was back, walking slowly and deliberately, looking pale and shaken.

Becky met her at the door and slipped an arm around her shoulders. "Ma, what's wrong? You seem absolutely peaked of late. I'm worried about you."

Hannah sat down at the kitchen table. She leaned forward, her head in her hands, her elbows resting on the table. "Oh, Becky," she spoke after a few moments. "I feel so foolish."

"Ma, what is it?"

"Truth be, I am embarrassed to tell you, but you're going to know sooner or later...." Tears filled her eyes as she choked out the words. "Becky, I'm with child!"

"Ma, you're what?" Her eyes widened in surprise and a smile started to spread across her face, even as she asked her mother to repeat herself. Had she really heard that right?

"I'm going to have a baby, which is ridiculous at my age. I am so ashamed. You must think your pa and I are a pair of old fools!"

"Ma, don't take on that way!" Becky could no longer hold back her own emotions. "We're going to have a new baby in this family? In this house? I can't believe it! When? This is so...." She stopped as she sought the right word. "It's so exciting!" She began to giggle but she quickly succumbed to gales of relieved laughter. "Oh, Ma!" She gasped for breath as her mother looked at her as if she'd lost her mind. "You have no idea! You really had me scared. All I could think of was how bad Mrs. Flaherty looked the last time I saw her and then you're sick, too, and I was afraid—" She stopped speaking to drop down in a chair next to her and put her hands over her mother's.

"I'm going to have a new baby sister or brother! I think it's wonderful!"

"Oh, Becky!" Her mother's tears returned. "That's sweet but I don't want to be an embarrassment to you. You should be getting married one day soon and having your own babies, and instead I'm having another. You must be thinking—" She took a deep breath but didn't say anything more.

"Ma, you don't need to be worrying about me! I ain't getting married to anybody for a long time yet and now I have a better reason than ever to be happy about being right here at home. A new baby! Make it a girl this time, won't you? I already have two ornery brothers. I need a baby sister!"

"Oh Becky, it's not as if I have a choice. We just take what we get. You know that!"

"Ma, I'm just teasing you. It don't matter. A new baby, boy or girl, will be so sweet to take care of. I can't wait! How soon?" She looked her mother full in the face.

"As best I can figure, this fall, September sometime." Her mother sniffed and pulled a lace-edged handkerchief out of her skirt pocket.

"September. Oh, Ma, this is going to be wonderful and so special." Becky was giddy with excitement.

"I am glad you're taking it so well." Hannah sat up straight and ran her hands over her long dark skirt.

"But Ma, why did you think I wouldn't? You know I love babies. How could you think I wouldn't be happy about this news?"

"Well it was quite a shock to me and your pa. I mean, I'm nearly thirty-eight years old. By the time I was your age, I'd already been married almost a year and Jacob was on his way. It just seems a shameful thing, a ridiculous thing now."

"Ma, I don't care what you say. You ain't old. You still look young and you don't act old at all. And I don't think you should be embarrassed. Pa neither. It means you're still young in the ways that count. It means Pa still loves you. I mean, really loves you!" Becky giggled again and gave her mother a quick embrace.

"Becky Darling!" Her mother blushed at the implication.

"Ma, it ain't like I don't know where babies come from after all. To me, it means Pa loves you as much as he ever did, and that is special. I know it is! That's why he looked at you so funny this morning when he was fussing about his job and mine."

An unintentional sigh escaped her mother. "He's worried. I know he is. There's this park business and his job and I was never sick like this with you or your brothers, but this time is different. Every day it seems all I can do is throw up. It'll be a wonder if this poor baby even gets enough to eat!" She sighed again and stood up, heading back to the loom.

"Ma, what can I make for you? You know, there is some smoked salt beef still out in the smokehouse. I could slice a little of it real thin and put it in some milk gravy. It would taste mighty fine over some hot buttered grilled bread. How does that sound?"

"It sounds pretty good," her mother admitted with a sheepish grin. "Especially if I don't have to cook it. Are you sure? I feel like you've enough to do around here already with the morning milking and your job—" She concentrated on the threads running up and down before her on the loom as she reached for the shuttle.

"Ma, it's fine, really. I can do it." Becky was on her feet, bustling around the kitchen, slicing the salt beef a few moments later when her little brother came in from school. He dropped two books strapped together near the front door and pulled his string bag of toy soldiers out from behind the loom where he'd pitched it before going to school.

"Hey, Benji," Becky greeted him. "How was school?"

"School is school." He shrugged and reached into the bag.

"Hold up there a minute," Becky redirected him. "Run down to the spring house and bring me that crock of milk I put in there this morning."

"Oh, Sis, I don't want to—"

"I didn't ask if you wanted to," Becky told him in no uncertain terms. "You can play with your soldiers in a little while. Right now you get down that hill and get me that milk, you hear?"

"You're not my boss, Becky. I don't have to do what you say."

"Benjamin Darling." His mother's voice quickly silenced his arguments. "Do what you were asked to do right now. There's no cause to be arguing."

Becky followed him to the door and bent down to spit in his ear. "It's for Ma, you dope. She don't feel good. Her tummy is bothering her and I'm making her some milk gravy, so don't be so grumpy."

He sighed. "All right. I'm a-going."

He returned momentarily, lugging a heavy stone crock.

"Thank you," his sister said with a matter-of-fact air. "And if you want Pa to be along without being in a bad mood a little later, you'd best get yourself outside and make sure you got hay ready for Maggie and Marge, before you start messing with toy soldiers." A welcoming sputter rose from the stove as she ladled milk into the hot cast iron skillet where she already had strips of dried beef sizzling in butter and flour.

Benji heaved a sigh in disgust and headed back out the door. Becky smiled in appreciation as he went. She milked in the morning, but Pa still milked at night, checking on the stock and making certain all was well each evening. It was Benji's job to have the hay ready so the cows could eat while the milking took place, making them more likely to stand still and be cooperative.

Becky spooned some of the gravy onto the homemade grilled toast and set it before her mother on the table. "Come on," she cajoled. "Enough with the loom today, or at least, for now."

While her mother took her first tentative bites, Becky sat down next to her and leaned back and let her eyes fall on the heavy oaken loom across the room. "Ma," Becky mused as her thoughts drifted back to the day's events now that her worries about her mother had been put to rest. "What do you really think of Miz Josie? I mean, she's a nice lady, don't you think?"

"Oh, Becky," her mother answered slowly, watching her daughter as she did. "Why do you ask?"

"Well, you know, I just find her so interesting. You should have heard her today, putting those mill workers in their place when they were fussing about this park business. And when Red Flaherty was not so nice to that photographer man, Mr. Thompson, she set him straight but in the sweetest way. She can tell them boys to straighten up but do it so nice, they don't even get mad. I think that's no small trick."

"You are certainly right about that." Hannah relaxed as the subject matter was less difficult than she anticipated. "The Bible says *a soft answer turneth away wrath.*"

"Red also talked about his mama. It sounds like she is really in a bad way. I know that is part of what had me so worried about you."

Her mother chuckled softly. "Well, that is certainly something to be thankful for, I suppose. Nothing wrong with me that another six months won't cure. Poor Mabel."

"Ma, what I don't understand is why some folks are so hateful about Miz Josie. I heard Mrs. Stone talking outside after church last Sunday, and she said how shameful Miz Josie is, living separate from her husband and getting a divorce and all and I just don't understand—"

"Rebecca, you know better than to be listening to gossip, and especially at church. That's even worse!" The milk gravy cure put a bit of her usual fire back into Hannah Darling's words. "Trudy McGillicuddy Stone should know better, too!"

"But Ma, why does she take on so—"

"Becky, there is no understanding why some folks carry on the way they do. Trudy McGillicuddy came into this valley and married Jonathan Stone years ago after he met her while visiting his cousins two counties over. She was a beautiful woman then, and she's still quite pretty, but she is unhappy and as far as I can tell, always has been. She's had a difficult life, there is no doubt. She came out from New York on one of them orphan trains years ago, as a half-grown girl."

"An orphan train? What is that? Is that why she talks so funny, because she's from New York?"

"Oh, I haven't heard anything of the trains for quite some time now," her mother mused, "but they were not so uncommon in years past. They would load up children from the orphanages and streets of New York City and send them west, out here to farm families in Indiana, Missouri, and Nebraska, any place where families might offer them a home and for many, a job."

"Really? What kind of a business was that?"

"It was really something, I can tell you. I was in Lebanon once, years ago when one of the trains came into town. They lined all the children up on the stage in the opera house and people went in and looked them over like they were buying a horse. They touched them and felt of their arms and legs to see if they were strong. I think the children here were lucky in that the local committee sponsoring the whole thing did their best to see to it that they went to good homes where they were fed and sent to school and cared for the way children should be."

She looked at her daughter, now more grown than not. "Not so in Trudy's case, as I understand it. The people who took her in were more interested in a free worker than in being kind to a little girl who needed it. It seems she had a little sister on that train as well and they were separated. Jonathan told your pa once that she has tried to find her but never could. It's a shame and I think it has colored her whole life. She's tried to make the rest of the world pay, it would seem, because she's so angry all the time." She finished her last bites of the toast, sopping up every bit of the gravy. "And yes, she still carries a bit of New York as well as an Irish brogue in her speech, but that's neither here nor there. It would make her more interesting to listen to if she wasn't so spiteful."

Becky shook her head, deep in thought. "I just can't imagine how hard that must have been."

"Nor can I." Then her mother added, "but this much I do know. Yes, Josie Smith is divorced, but no one knows what really goes on in another's home. Just like her mama, Josie has buried babies and there is nothing more heart-breaking for any woman in this life. Whatever else she may or may not have done, she treats this family well, hiring you and buying butter, milk, eggs and rugs from us for her hotel, so I can tell you this. There will be no one speaking badly of Josie Smith under this roof and especially not when we're taking her money. I won't have it! You understand me?"

"Yes, ma'am," Becky answered smartly, while smiling on the inside. Sassy indeed. She leaned over and wrapped her arms around her mother one more time. Hannah quickly clasped her arms around her daughter's.

"Thank you, Becky," she added with a soft sigh.

"For a little gravy? That was easy, Ma."

"No, for so much more than that." Hannah Darling patted the arms that still surrounded her. "For reminding me." She slid a hand across her own belly. "For reminding me that it is a wise woman who knows when she has the good fortune to be blessed. Blessed with a good husband and a good daughter as well as a couple of foolish sons!"

"Who's a foolish son?" Zeb Darling asked as he swung the door open wide and stepped inside.

Chapter 3

"Hmmm." Hannah Darling eyed her husband with a hint of mischief flirting across her face. "Who? Who? Who? Your feet don't fit no limb."

"Do you see the way she talks to me?" He turned to Becky in mock distress, and his daughter was thankful that he seemed to be in a much more amiable frame of mind than this morning. "All I asked was who's a foolish son?"

"Oh, I imagine your mama thought of you that way more than once," his wife answered again.

"Could be, could be." He grinned and his glance took in their faces and the empty plate still on the table. "Eating in the middle of the afternoon are we, girls?" His eyes settled on Hannah. "So did you tell her?"

"I did," she answered.

"So what do you think?" He swung a full milk bucket inside the door and sat it on the floor next to Becky.

"Oh, Pa, I think it's wonderful!" Becky gushed again. "A new---"

He put a finger to his lips and jerked his eyes towards her brother, who had come in with him and was once again on the floor with his tin soldiers.

"Oh!" She was instantly quiet and turned to find another large glass jar. She placed a clean dry cloth over the mouth of it and glanced sideways at her father. She whispered back, "why?"

"Some things just need to be told in their own good time and there's no great need to hurry them along." Zebulon Darling had a strong philosophical side to his personality which he generally kept hidden from much of the world, Becky knew, but from time to time it crept out. How else could they have ended up with a dog named Homer and a cat called Shakespeare? At her mother's insistence she studied the Bible, and at her father's, she had read several of the works of Shakespeare. She liked *Romeo and Juliet* the best, as well as *A Midsummer Night's Dream.*

She silently surveyed her father as he stood fondly watching his youngest stretched out on the rug.

"So who's winning down there?" he asked.

"Pa." Benji looked up with a grin. "Who always wins? It's General Black Jack Pershing who beats the Kaiser's soldiers. You know that."

"Yes, I know that." He continued to watch for a few more moments.

Slowly, Becky began to pour the rich liquid from the bucket through the cloth into the jar, the only processing this milk would see before it was turned into cream, butter and milk for sale to the hotel, other neighbors, or simply used by the Darling family.

"Benji," she called to the miniature general on the rug as he marshaled his troops. "There's cream here with what I've got saved from the last couple of days that'll need churning to make butter for tomorrow. You start and I'll finish it."

"All right," he replied without enthusiasm, looking first at her and then at both of his parents in turn as he dragged himself to his feet. He didn't even bother to protest with all three present.

She finished transferring the cream into a three quart stoneware jar with its wooden lid that fit under the black machinery of the butter churn. "Here you go." She gave the crank half a turn and listened to the dasher splash about in the cream.

"So what's new in the hotel business, Missy?" her father asked as he sat down at the far end of the table and began to look through a handful of papers he had brought in earlier. Her father often called her Missy since he said she was the only Miss in the entire household. She liked the nickname when he was in a good mood, like now, but not so much when he was argumentative like this morning, and it often changed to Miss Priss.

"Oh, not so much," she answered as she stepped to the large metal sink on the far side of the stove and began to pump water to rinse the milk bucket. Her father had installed an inside-the-house hand pump last year and it made her feel as if they were a very up-to-date household now. It was not like the running water that Miz Josie had at the hotel or what her friend Georgia McCandles had in her house in Lebanon but her father was a doctor, after all. Still, it was quite the modern convenience and so much easier than pumping well water outside or worse, hauling water from the spring as so many area families still had to do.

"Red Flaherty said that his mama wasn't doing very good, just wasting away really. And Mr. Fredericks, the traveling salesman, he's come and gone again. There's also a Mr. Thompson, a photographer, staying with us right now. Did I tell you about him? He said he was inspired by William Lenz' pictures of this whole valley from a few years ago. He also said he was taking photographs of lots of different mills for one of the magazines on account of the grist mills aren't doing as much business as they used to and well, you shoulda heard Red Flaherty's answer to that! He didn't waste no time telling this poor photographer man that nobody around here wanted to hear none of that." She chuckled in the re-telling of the story, finding more humor in it than she had originally.

"I don't doubt that." Her father nodded absent-mindedly, his focus remaining on the papers in front of him.

"Pa, what is that you're studying so?" Becky asked.

"Danged if I know." Zeb sat back in exasperation. "Some kind of documents from the government that Harold Larkin, the mail carrier from over in Dallas County, got a holt of. He said they told how the Federal government went about making a park out there at Yellowstone in Wyoming all those years ago. I thought maybe if I studied up on it some, I could figure out how they done it and how we could stop it here at Bennett Spring, before the whole place gets sold out from under us."

"Pa!" Becky stopped what she was doing to stare open-mouthed at her father.

"What? Daughter, what do you expect? You think I'm just going to sit here and let this thing happen without putting up a fight?"

"I just never thought...." Her voice trailed off.

"Never thought what? That I'd do something about it?"

"I just never thought you'd do something so...so sneaky!" She let the word out and then immediately clapped her hand over her mouth as if it had escaped without her consent.

"Sneaky? Did you really call me sneaky? Under-handed? Is that what you really think of your father?!"

"No, Pa, that's not what I meant. I just—"

"Hannah!" Zeb bellowed at the top of his lungs as if his wife wasn't practically within arm's reach, let alone within immediate earshot.

"Becky, apologize to your father," her mother commanded in a surprisingly soft voice from her seat at the loom.

"Pa, I'm sorry." Becky was immediately contrite. "I didn't mean no disrespect but I don't know if you can stop this thing, and I'm not sure you should, even if you could. Besides all that, Miz Josie said today, it might not even happen!"

"Oh, she did, did she?" Zeb leaned back in his chair, with the two front feet completely off the floor, arms folded across his chest.

"Yes, when Red Flaherty asked her about it at dinner time, she laughed and asked him if he could really imagine the state government putting out money for such a thing. She told me later, after everybody was gone, that it might not even happen."

"From her lips to God's ear," Zebulon Darling muttered under his breath as began to gather his papers and bundle them together to clear the table.

* * * * * *

The spring days sped past as Becky found herself lost in the business of laundry--at the hotel as well as at home-- milking, cooking, setting tables and clearing dirty dishes, changing beds, and all the other myriad of daily tasks that went along with the running of a small hotel and keeping pace with her own family. Her mother's morning sickness had finally eased but her energy level was still not what it had once been. Even so, Becky noticed that despite her mother's initial conflict over the impending arrival of another Darling, she now practically glowed when she talked or smiled. Becky thought she had never seen her look more radiant. Her newfound beauty was not lost on her husband either. Concern for his wife and the new little one on the way, while a constant on his mind, still did not dampen his determination to find a way to stop the possible coming of the new park.

For her part, Becky did her best to avoid the topic altogether when her father was around. It affected her deeply to be at odds with him on any subject and she was determined not to allow this difference of opinion, no matter how profound, to become a major stumbling block between them. One glorious spring day after another, each drenched in the ever-increasing warmth of the sun, seemed to run into the next as she scurried back and forth between the Brice Inn and home.

She had taken an afternoon earlier in the season to go hunting for morels, and she and Benji had found a bagful further up the valley. She had carefully cleaned them, dredged them in flour and fried them one evening for a special treat for them all.

She had kept a careful eye on the budding trees and helped her father plant corn in their garden when, as Granny Trundle reminded her, "when the oak tree leaves were the size of a squirrel's ear." She had even managed to get up to Granny and Grampy Trundle's cabin one evening before dark to take them some extra butter and cheese. As always, they were most appreciative. She knew Pa saw them regularly, swinging wide on his postal route every chance he got, even though they only got one letter a month from their son in Texas, but she still liked to get up and see them whenever she could.

They weren't her real grandparents, just an elderly couple who had been kind to her father when he had first come here. When he needed a place to stay, they had allowed him to live with them, once Hannah Andersen had caught his eye. Their only son, Terry, had settled in Texas after serving overseas in the Great War, but they continued to live far up in the woods more than a mile above the spring. Pa had bought his land from them, land that they had once hoped to give to their son. And in a way, they had done just that. Pa treated them as well as any son could have and they often told her so when she stopped by to visit.

Finally, on a particularly fine Ozarks day, Becky managed to get away from the Brice Inn a bit early one afternoon. She had but one thought on her mind as she scampered towards the house on the far side of the spring.

"What's the big hurry?" her little brother asked as she came up the trail.

"Going fishing," she told him, crossing the porch in two steps. She reached into the rafters to pull down her favorite cane pole.

"Can I come?" He scooped up the toy soldiers he'd been playing with, now that his battlefield had transitioned from the living room rug to the front porch with the coming of warmer weather.

"I don't know. Can you?" She echoed back. "Did you ask Ma? Have you got a pole that's ready? What are you supposed to be doing that you haven't yet?" She peppered him with questions.

"Oh, I dunno, but I can ask Ma quick." She sat down on the front step to look over her pole and stretch out the line. She'd worked on it earlier in the week so it would be ready when she got the chance to actually go. She had found that while she did enjoy this business of working for a living, it took up a great deal more time than she would ever have imagined including valuable fishing time. She shook her head with a smile as her brother practically kicked in the front door in his enthusiasm.

Her mother appeared at the door a few moments later. "Where you going, Becky? He wants to know if he can go, too, but that's really up to you."

"I'm off to the river, Ma," Becky spoke without looking up from her pole. "I don't mind if he comes, you know that, but—" she looked up sharply at her brother. "You gotta do what I say, understand? No back talk and no arguing. Agreed?"

"Yes, Becky, I promise." He stood so straight and serious, it made her want to laugh.

"All right, but what about a pole? Are you going to fish or just get underfoot?"

"I won't get under your feet, Becky. I promise." He nodded solemnly. "I had a pole last year but I'm not sure where it is now."

"I'm sure you're not." Becky smiled patiently at her mother and stood up to reach into the rafters a second time to pull down another cane pole. She had prepared it as well, expecting that she wouldn't be going alone.

"Come on with you then, but you got to carry your own pole and be willing to dig worms, you understand?"

"Yes, Becky," he replied.

"You two be careful and watch him around the water, Becky. That's the only thing I worry about with the two of you down there by the confluence. I don't need him falling in and drowning and—"

"It'll be all right, Ma. I'll watch him. I promise." Becky kissed her mother on the cheek. Despite having grown up at Bennett Spring, anything to do with the water always scared her mother. The father of one of her childhood friends had drowned years ago and she had never forgotten it.

She walked down the road, Benji trudging along at her side, each with a cane pole in hand. Becky also carried a small canvas tote that had a few spare hooks in a pocket in the front, some fishing line, and a miniature garden spade inside. She's found she could dig worms and fill the whole bag with them and a bit of damp earthy cover and that would keep her happily occupied on the river bank for quite some time.

Many of the locals, as well as visitors to the area, happily tossed a line into the spring branch, but for fishing Becky preferred the confluence, the place where the spring waters joined the Niangua River. She could fish anywhere along the spring branch or the river and often had, with her father or with Jake and his friends. Years ago, she remembered, the whole family would go together. Lately, it seemed someone was always too busy, her father with his postal route, which continued to expand the longer he worked it. Whether it was a case of new people moving into the area or more people finding the mail delivery to be more reliable and therefore, something they used more frequently, she wasn't sure. She just knew that there were always more letters than ever that needed to be delivered.

Benji kicked the occasional large piece of gravel as they walked along, sending them bouncing down the road ahead of them.

"Hey!" Becky hollered at him as one of them took a sideways twist and nearly hit her in the ankle.

"Sorry, Sis." Benji grinned his apology.

He scampered ahead and stopped to stare at the water falling over the crib dam. What was it about the water cascading over the man-made barrier, creating its own waterfall? Everyone loved to simply watch the frothy white purity of the constantly moving water as it poured over the dam, hit bottom and flowed on down the spring branch, through the gentle twists and turns, blue-green waters moving swiftly, surely towards their end destination, the river.

They were halfway to their favorite fishing spot, about to pass by the Brice Inn and the town as a whole, when Benji looked up. "Well, lookey there!" He stopped kicking rocks to stare over the rail fence.

A dazzling display of automotive engineering was parked beside the Brice Inn, a much newer model than the converted vehicle that Becky had ridden in a few weeks before with Jake. The sleek black finish reflected the afternoon sunshine, as did the spotless chrome hood ornament and trim around the headlights. There were four doors, a fold down top and two beautifully upholstered black seats, one in front and another full one in the back.

"Who does that belong to?" Benji asked in wide-eyed breathless wonder.

"I have no idea." Becky was as bedazzled as her little brother at the site of the gorgeous touring car parked here in little old Brice, but she did her best not to let it show.

"Becky, you know everybody that comes to the Brice Inn, don'tcha?" Benji's understanding of his sister's employment was that she would undoubtedly know such things without even being asked.

"Not if they arrived after I got off work, you sap!" she snapped back.

"Well, why don't you go in and ask?" The solution to the question seemed simple enough to an eleven-year-old.

"You expect me to just go in and find Miz Josie and demand to know who's driving that fancy car?"

"It would seem to be the easiest way, wouldn't it?"

Becky whirled at the sound of the voice coming from behind them. A distractingly handsome young man, only a few years older than her, had approached from the water's edge. They had both been so busy admiring the flashy new car they had not noticed him until he spoke.

"Oh, my apologies." He started over when he caught the look of surprise and consternation on her face. "I didn't mean to startle you. I went down to take a look at the water. What a beautiful place this is! Do you live close by?"

"Yep, we live right down the road there a-piece." Benji began to point the way until his sister grabbed him by the shoulder and gave him a pinch. "Oww! Becky!"

"You don't need to be tellin' strangers everything there is to know, first thing!" She snapped at him under her breath. "Hello." She turned back to the young man in the cream-colored suit with a powder blue shirt underneath that matched his cornflower blue eyes. "Yes, we live here. You visiting the inn?"

"I am." He immediately shook the hand of the hesitant eleven-year-old boy in an open, friendly gesture and then promptly extended the same hand to the young lady at his side who was nearly as tentative. "My name is J.C. Shine from Holt's Summit, near Jefferson City. Perhaps you've heard of it. I'm here for a few days with Senator Clarence Wiggins to look over the area and do some interviews with local folks."

"Uh, well, my name is Becky, Rebecca." She managed a reply despite the sudden tightening in her throat. "This is my brother, Benji."

"Ben," her little brother corrected her.

Becky noticed he didn't seem to have any difficulty speaking for himself in front of this tall eloquent stranger. She was irritated, scrambling mentally trying to figure out what had happened to her own voice. She met strangers all the time, working the desk at the inn. Why should this one be any different?

"I actually work at the inn during the day. I'm not at work right now. What I mean is..." She stumbled over her words even more than before.

"I can see that." He smiled, revealing even more boyish charm, Becky thought, as he nodded towards their fishing poles.

"Is that your automobile?" Benji asked without hesitation.

"Well, yes and no. It is the one I drove to get here today, but it doesn't belong to me. She's a beauty, isn't she? Would you like to take a closer look?"

"Yeah!" Benji tossed his pole onto the ground, but he managed only a step towards the car before Becky took him in hand.

"Not now, Benji!" She snapped. "We got other business to 'tend to."

"Oh, yeah, we're going fishing at the confluence." He cast a last longing glance towards the car but minded his sister and retrieved his fishing pole.

"The confluence?"

"Where the spring branch meets the river down below." Becky gave a quick bob of her head in the direction they had been heading.

"Oh, I see." He gazed off into the distance as if he could actually see what she was talking about even though it was a half mile away. His eyes quickly returned to her despite the vaguely quizzical expression on his face.

She could think of no simple explanation that would clarify the situation and she wasn't even certain that she wanted to make one, regardless. Who was he anyway? She'd heard what he'd said but it didn't make it any clearer to her, who he was or why he was here. All she could think was that she and her brother ought to be moving on. This stranger, whoever he was, made her feel awkward and shy, all the things she thought she had finally left behind as a result of working, making her own way in the world. A few words from this good-looking man in a fine suit, who had apparently arrived in this fancy car, and she felt like a foolish little girl again who knew little of the world outside her own valley.

She nudged Benji from behind and they started down the road again. "It was nice to meet you," Becky managed to toss back over her shoulder as they walked away. "Oh," she turned back, her feet still moving as she walked backwards, "you said interviews. What kind of interviews?"

"About the park," he called back. "Interviews about whether this," he suddenly threw his hands up over his head and then lowered them to shoulder level as he made a quarter turn towards the flowing water behind him, "should become Missouri's first state park!"

Chapter 4

Fishing that afternoon had not turned out to be nearly as enjoyable as she had imagined all week long. Her favorite spot to dig for worms was along the bank, near the small eddy where they usually fished. It was located a short distance above the confluence, but it was drier than she had expected and the soil was hard. Good fishing worms were not going to be as readily available as usual, and the whole business made her cross and stole the joy from her highly anticipated fishing trip.

"What did that feller mean, interviews for the park?" Benji asked after a few minutes of watching his sister struggle with the spade and come up with little for her efforts.

"How am I supposed to know that?" Becky answered his question with a question. "I guess he's going to ask people if they think it is a good idea or not to make a park here at Brice." She snorted at the idea. "If'n he asks Pa, he'll get an earful, or Red Flaherty too, for that matter." She stood up straight from the stooped digging position and tossed down the spade. "Here, you try. Right there." She pointed to the spot she was interested in with an outstretched foot. "I'm going to put one of these scrawny river worms on this hook and see if I can find me an interested catfish. No need for this afternoon to be a total waste of time." She snatched up her cane pole and got down to business.

Benji picked up the spade and began to pick at the ground under the bank, carefully easing out the rocks and working the soil around them.

"So what if people tells him they want it or what if they tells him they don't?" Benji seemed to be thinking aloud as much as anything else. "What difference will that make?"

"I don't have any idea!" Becky's retort was sharper than she intended, and silenced her brother who simply continued to dig with no further comment. He knew exactly what he was digging for—long, red river worms and not the green-tinged ones, either, because they had a stink to them. The red ones were tougher and would stay on the hook better than their green cousins. Besides, the fish could tell the difference. He and Becky were convinced of that. Catfish definitely preferred the red ones.

Everything about this park business was beginning to get on Becky's nerves. She found herself tiptoeing verbally, being careful about everything she said around her father these days. She had never felt that way before and she didn't like it. She had always felt free and easy in her own home, discussing whatever she wished with her parents for as long as she could remember. It was a completely different situation when she visited her friend, Georgia, in town a couple of times a year. They had met at the Brice Church of God and become almost instant friends. Dr. and Mrs. McCandles were always nice to her at church and at their home, too, but the moment she entered there, she could feel the difference. There was an unspoken understanding that many things were simply not open to discussion. At times, Becky could admit, at least to herself, that she envied Georgia's lavish home with luxuries like running water and even a system of pipes that allowed her father to talk from his office to the kitchen and tell the cook and servants what he wanted and when. Georgia's closet in her bedroom was filled with fine clothes and more pairs of shoes than Becky thought she might ever own in a lifetime. Her own house was comfortable but modest by comparison, but there was also a freedom and a joy there that she had never felt in Georgia's home. As a result, she knew, given the choice, she would never trade places with her friend even if that were possible. But now, that seemed to have changed, all because of this park business. And her father wasn't the only one who was struggling with it.

The mill workers were uneasy in a way she'd never noticed before, and many like Red said so. Others just stared sullenly, watching and listening to the conversations that continued to swirl, at the inn, at the Bennett store, the blacksmith's shop, both the grist mill and the saw mill, even at church. Anywhere people gathered. *"Where two or more are gathered in my name,"* the bit of scripture from Matthew popped into Becky's head, *"there will I be also."*

Well, this didn't seem to have anything to do with the good Lord or his encouragement or anything else that was good and blessed and holy.

She had been totally enthusiastic about the idea of a park in the beginning and she still was, but she had to admit it didn't come without headaches. The idea of the end of the town of Brice did not set well with her despite what Miz Josie had said that day at dinner. The end of the post office and Pa's postal route was especially disturbing. What else would they have to give up to have this park in their midst? And if there was no town of Brice, then there would be no Brice Inn. If that was gone, then what was the point of having more people come to stay and visit? No hotel surely meant no hotel guests. She was so deep in her musings that she almost missed the bite on her line.

"Whoa, here we go!" She jerked the line and felt it tug back, assuring her she had hooked her quarry. She lifted the pole and pulled in the line by hand, and landed the pan-sized catfish on the bank.

"Wow, that's what we want!" Benji jumped out of the way and then immediately reached down to wrap his hand around the back side of the fish's head so as to avoid the catfish's famous spines tucked around its lower jaw.

"That's a nice one, Becky!" Her brother's admiring tone helped to bring her out of her doldrums. "We got him now!" Benji pulled a piece of twine from the back pocket of his overalls and expertly threaded it through the fish's gills and out its mouth. "I bet he goes a pound and a half!" he exclaimed as he held up the flat-head cat for his sister to take in its full length.

"Good enough." Becky nodded as a smile of satisfaction spread across her face. "Let's see if we can come up with another one or two. Some of Ma's cornbread and fresh catfish, you can't do better than that for supper." She looked over to where her brother had been patiently working the soil. "How you doing for worms?"

"Becky, they're in there. You just got to sort of coax 'em out." Benji reached in and pulled a handful of long, wriggling worms from the satchel she carried earlier.

"You got more patience for it than me today, that's for sure." Becky nodded as she surveyed the boy's handiwork.

"It ain't hard. You just gotta feel for the worms, I guess. Girls ain't usually real fond of worms, anyway." He sounded so grown up in his assumptions that it made her smile.

"And where did you learn that?" She couldn't help but ask.

"At school." He answered with a matter-of-fact attitude that simply begged for the next question.

"At school? In Miz Bailey's classroom?"

"No, silly," he giggled. "Junior Thompson put a worm down the back of Loretta Gordon's dress and she didn't like it one bit!"

Becky's laughter burst out, a welcome relief from her tensions of the last many days. She wiped away a tear with the back of her hand and her brother peered up at her from where he sat on the gravel, working a worm onto a fishing hook.

"You all right, Becky?" he asked, wondering why certain girls found some things so amusing while others definitely did not. Junior Thompson must have had it right. That same day he'd gotten in so much trouble, he confided to Benji, "Girls are weird."

His thoughts meandered back to the local interest in the park. "So, you want the park but Pa doesn't? Who's right?"

Becky admired her younger brother's ability to cut to the chase, simply bypassing the complications that bogged down all the adults involved.

She sighed before answering. "It ain't that simple, Benji. If'n it was, there would be nothing to argue about. It's more like I'm thinking of the future," she paused as she realized her explanation to the youngest Darling was helping to put her own thoughts in order, "and Pa is thinking of the way things have always been and how he doesn't want them to change."

"Do you want stuff to change? Don't you like the way it is now?"

"Oh, Benji, nobody gets to make that choice, not really. Stuff is going to change. It's kinda like that car and the ones we're starting to see more often around here."

He looked at her solemnly trying to understand the explanation she was making.

"We're seeing more cars all the time, aren't we? And some folks, they don't like them. They say they're noisy and unreliable and that all that oil and gasoline smells bad. They say they'll never give up their horses and wagons and buggies or even mules or oxen, but I'm a-telling you, Benji, automobiles are here and they ain't a-going away. Even Jake was driving one the other day."

"He was?" His eyes brightened at the mention of his beloved older brother. Jake was only a year older than Becky and in many ways she had always looked up to him, but Benji adored him and everything he did. "When? Where? How come I didn't get to see it?"

"Oh, calm down, it wasn't his or anything. He borried it from a friend of his, but he drove it past the Brice Inn just after I got off work and he gave me a ride in it for a little ways. You were still in school is all. I'm sure you'll see him another day before long, driving some fancy car."

"Oh, shucks! I wished I'd have been there. Maybe he'll get him an auto like that one we seen by the Brice Inn. Wouldn't that be something, Becky?"

"Yeah, that would be something." She answered without enthusiasm, as concern for how he might obtain such a vehicle overshadowed her other thoughts.

They caught two more catfish and, just as she hoped, Ma made a delicious supper for them all. As she cleared the dishes from the table, she thought about what her work day would be like tomorrow and for the first time, she realized she was dreading it. Thoughts of a handsome young man in a cream-colored linen suit danced through her thoughts.

"What's wrong with you?" Her mother frowned at Becky as she dropped the dishes into the sink in a careless manner.

"What? I...what do you mean? I'm sorry. I guess I'm just tired." She tried to avoid giving an answer to a question she didn't even understand herself.

"Well, of course you are." The concern in her mother's voice made her feel worse, not better, as if she was guilty of some secret sin. "You work all day and then go fishing and now you're doing dishes. I'm not much help around here at the moment, I fear." Despite her words, Hannah Darling still sat at the table, lingering over her coffee.

"Ma, you're fine, really. And so am I. I guess I was just thinking I have a lot to do tomorrow at Miz Josie's. It's a laundry day and I got sheets and towels to wash and hang out is all, but it will be all right. At least she's got that wringer washer now and real running water, so that makes it a lot easier to fill that tub and get everything washed and rinsed." She hoped the lie sounded convincing as she tried to persuade herself as well as her mother.

"Well, don't work too hard, you hear?" She smiled lovingly at her daughter. "Save some energy for times like today when you can just take off and go fishing. You deserve it, that's for certain."

A part of her wanted to dawdle the next morning, putting off the inevitable, running into that troublesome new guest. She knew, however, an early start would be best with the amount of work she had waiting. That was it, she decided as she walked along, looking for the mink, who was not there this morning. She would just concentrate on her work. Surely he wouldn't be around where she would be doing laundry.

A muskrat swam from one side of the stream to the other in his funny unique way with only his nose above the surface, parting the waters in a V-shape. While most days she would have enjoyed the sight, her thoughts were elsewhere. Just concentrate on the work, she told herself again, and that will get you through the day.

"Good morning, Miss Becky," Josie greeted her, coffee pot in hand, from the table where she was serving in the parlor. "Come meet these gentlemen." She waved her over.

"This is State Senator Clarence Wiggins and his aide, J.C. Shine, from Jefferson City. They're going to be here with us for a few days. The Senator is head of the new Tourism Committee and they are here to look us over, so to speak, and interview folks and see about making this park into a reality."

"Gents, this is Miss Becky Darling. Her family lives up the way and I don't mind telling you she has been a godsend to me this last year. A very valuable employee here at the Brice Inn. If you need anything at all and you don't see me right away, I'm sure Becky can help you."

"Good morning, young lady," the senator responded first and shook her hand, reaching across a plate of fried eggs, ham and hashed browned potatoes.

"Good morning," Becky answered.

"It's good to see you again." J.C. smiled as he, too, took her hand. "We met yesterday," he informed the other two, "but she was on a mission with her brother, I believe."

"Oh?" Josie Smith, who prided herself on knowing all that was going on in the valley, raised an eyebrow in surprise at this news.

"So how did you do last night?" he asked. "Catch anything?"

"Yes." A small smile escaped Becky despite her earlier resolve. "We caught three catfish."

"That sounds good. I can't wait to try my hand at it later, of course."

"You fish?" she asked.

"A little," he answered. "I hear the trout fishing is good here. That's what these spring waters are famous for, right?"

"Trout, yes, and lots of other good fish. I'd best get to work. It was good to meet you all. Miz Josie." Becky made a quick nod to all three and turned back towards the front desk.

She found they had another new guest besides the senator and his aide. The front desk register showed a Mr. Lee Taylor had arrived from St. Louis and that reminded Becky she had noticed another car parked outside. As she bundled up laundry to take to the back, she and Josie crossed paths which gave her a chance to ask about him.

"He came in late, after dark," Josie noted. "Driving these roads is hard enough in the daylight, let alone at night." She shook her head. "He said he was looking for a place to rest but to be honest, I couldn't tell if he meant for a night or for a week. He looked so tired last night I tried not to ask him much. Come to think of it, he didn't even come down for breakfast this morning. I'll check on him in a little while if we don't see him before long."

Becky soon found herself up to her elbows in wash and rinse water and then busy stringing sheets out along the back line to dry, after running each piece individually through a hand-crank wringer. Dinner time came quickly but she was glad to have the washing done by then. All she would have to do later in the afternoon was to pull down the dried sheets, fold them and pack them along with their fresh scent of sunshine into the back linen closet.

As she laid out the table service for the noon meal, she found a new diner in the parlor. "Today's dinner is ham and beans and cornbread," she announced to the mustached man, seated alone at the corner table.

"That's a might strange for breakfast," he commented softly, "but it will do fine."

"Oh, you must be Mr. Taylor." The revelation popped out before she could stop it.

A gentle smile crossed his face. "That's right. How did you know?"

Becky's face flushed as she tried to cover her lack of discretion. "Oh, I'm sorry. It's just that most people around here don't stay in bed much after the sun rises, not that that's a bad thing, mind you. I'm sorry. I didn't mean…"

His smile broadened but Becky noticed as she looked up in embarrassment that it did not reach the sadness that still surrounded his hazel eyes. "It's fine, really. I'm sure you are right. Hard-working people need to get up in the morning, ready to make hay while the sun shines, don't they? And I usually do too, but that bed upstairs was so comfortable and it was a long trip. The whole point of my stop here is to get some rest, so it seemed a fit way to begin."

"You don't have to explain it all to me," Becky continued to apologize. "It surely wasn't my aim to criticize. I'd be happy to ask the cook to make you some eggs or hot cereal or something more fittin' for breakfast, if you like."

"No need, no need." He dismissed the idea with a wave of his hand. "Beans and ham and cornbread will be just fine. I would like a big glass of milk with that, if possible."

"Yes sir." Becky grinned as the awkward moment had passed. "I can take care of that. And there is chocolate cake for dessert today."

"Well, now, you cannot ask for better than that!" Lee Taylor looked like a man who was on his way to enjoying a good beginning to his vacation, Becky thought as she walked towards the kitchen.

George Thompson, the photographer, and the senator and his aide soon joined him in the dining room. There were no mill workers today, Becky noticed, and she wondered if they had caught word of the purpose of the senator's mission there and had made a deliberate decision to stay away. After thinking about it for a moment or two, however, she thought it probably had as much to do with the day's menu as anything else. Beans and cornbread was about as common as food got in this part of the country and many would bring that sort of fare from home and eat it cold, rather than to pay for it in a restaurant, even the local inn.

William Sherman Bennett came over from the store and picked up a bowl of beans and some cornbread wrapped in a small cloth and carried them back to the store to eat his meal there as he often did. He greeted the senator and his aide but he did not tarry in the parlor and hurried back to work.

Josie and Becky sat down to their dinner as usual at the table closest to the kitchen. A few moments later, George Thompson stood up and stopped at their table to sign a dinner ticket for his room.

"Miz Josie, I just have another day or so left here," he commented, "and I've taken all the mill pictures I was sent here to get. I've photographed the spring and most of the length of the spring branch, still I was wondering. Do you have any ideas, any secret places, so to speak, that you might suggest would make an extraordinary photograph before I go? It is such a beautiful area that I feel like I want to take as much of it with me as I can."

Josie leaned back from the table with a smile at the compliment to her home valley. "Well, sir, I don't pretend to know a thing about those cameras you boys all tote around, but if'n it was me, I think some of the prettiest views of this valley are the ones from above, like over on the trail along the bluff. Have you been up there?"

"No, I'm not sure how to get there from here. Where would be the best place…" He hesitated as he looked out the parlor window.

"It's on the other side of the spring branch, of course," she laughed, "and it will take a little walking carrying all your equipment, but it should not be so hard to find. I tell you what, Becky could show you."

"That would be really helpful, if you can spare her."

"Oh, she's worked plenty hard already today, doing the hardest job around here as far as I'm concerned. Becky, you don't mind to show Mr. Thompson along the bluff trail, do you? You know where I mean, the place just before it rounds the curve up there, you get the best look at the spring branch and really the whole town."

"Yes, ma'am!" Becky jumped at the chance to go hiking the bluff trail rather than house chores. "I know exactly where the best views are from up there. I can take him. Are you ready to go now?" She tossed her napkin onto the table and started to get up.

"No, no," the photographer laughed. "Not quite yet. I've got a couple of things to attend to first. I'll go check my camera and bag and figure out exactly what I need so I'm not carrying any more than necessary. Give me a half hour or so. Will that be acceptable?"

"More than acceptable, sir," Josie answered for her. She looked back at Becky. "You finish your dinner before you go running off. You'll need the energy, heaven knows!"

Mr. Thompson headed up the stairs and Becky reached for the piece of chocolate cake still waiting for her. She did have to admit she looked forward to it, as nobody could lay down a layer of chocolate fudge frosting like Miz Josie.

"Excuse me." Her attention was diverted from the chocolate as J.C. Shine leaned over from his table. "I couldn't help but overhear. You're going to guide that photographer along one of the bluffs, you said. Would you mind if I tagged along? The senator has some legislative paperwork he's going to attend to this afternoon and I thought, if it's all right, I'd get another view from up above, as you put it."

"Well, I--" Becky tried to think of a plausible excuse but the chance to do so was quickly taken out of her hands.

"Of course she doesn't mind." Josie stood up, gathering dirty dishes as she headed towards the kitchen. "Might as well escort two handsome men as one!"

Chapter 5

Becky felt like the last bite of chocolate cake was permanently stuck in her throat. Now what? was all she could think. She was trapped into taking along that irritating flatlander, as her father often called the folks who came from outside the area. He was probably some citified knot head who couldn't even walk trails without falling down or getting hurt. Just what she needed, playing guide and nursemaid, no doubt, to a knot head of a flatlander.

Despite her misgivings, she was standing on the porch within the agreed upon thirty minutes as was Mr. Thompson. He had pared his equipment down to one tall camera on its tripod, folded and on his shoulder, and a medium-sized leather bag.

The senator's aide appeared at the front door, in a page boy's flat cap, short pants and long socks. He immediately volunteered to carry the photographer's bag. "I don't mind at all," he said as he grabbed it up.

"Well, I'm not getting any younger, son," George Thompson said with half a chuckle, "so I'm not about to argue with you. Where are we off to, young lady?" He turned his attention to Becky who had quickly looked the other way to keep from laughing out loud at the sight of J.C. Shine's naked knees. Men in her neck of the woods always wore long pants, with the possible exception of deliberately getting into the water. As cold as the local spring waters were, however, even at the confluence with the mixing of the spring and warmer river water, it was the rare gent who purposely entered the water except in an emergency or on a purely accidental basis.

"You work as a professional photographer then? You travel a great deal, do you?" J.C. managed to keep up a running conversation even as they hiked along, Becky noticed. Not bad, she thought, seeing as how she had set a brisk pace and he was also carrying the photographer's load.

She took them along the road towards the foot bridge between the dam and the confluence. While she had crossed by foot on the flange bridge, she couldn't imagine getting across there carrying this kind of equipment, and the foot bridge across the crib dam wouldn't be much better. One little stumble and one of her two charges would quickly be in the frigid spring branch below. She thought about walking them all the way to the wider wooden roadway bridge near the confluence but that seemed so far out of the way. Surely, the foot bridge, halfway between the confluence and the town of Brice, would work.

"Yes, ever since before the Great War," Mr. Thompson managed to answer. "Back then, I worked for a couple different newspapers back East and they had me all over Europe. Pretty heady stuff, but dangerous, and by the end, just plain exhausting. These days the magazines are starting to pay nearly as well and it's a lot more pleasant than war, crime or racing after fire engines, if you know what I mean."

J.C. laughed and Becky couldn't help but notice it was a truly joyous sound. "I can imagine. I think I wouldn't mind a job that paid me to go to places like this on a regular basis."

"Have you done a lot of traveling yourself?" Mr. Thompson inquired as he struggled a bit to keep pace.

"I guess I would have to answer, yes, although much of it was my father's doing, not mine." The younger man answered with a nonchalance that surprised her. "I was born in St. Louis where my father was a dam and locks engineer, but by the time I was ten, he'd picked up the whole family and moved us to the Panama Canal Zone where he worked in the construction of the locks there. I have three older brothers so it was quite an adventure for all of us, the years we spent there. After that, he got involved in a venture in Cuba as the owner of a couple of hotels. I really loved life there and would have happily stayed, but my father contracted malaria in Panama and despite the best doctors available both there and in Cuba, he could not get well and stay well. Back in St. Louis he continued to have health problems until my mother insisted on taking him back to his parents' farm near Holt's Summit. Moving him out of the city seemed to do him more good than anything else."

"I can appreciate that," Mr. Thompson stated as they approached the bridge. The narrow wooden structure, slung low between the two sides of the spring branch, accommodated single file traffic and had no hand rails of any kind. Like so many other man-made structures along the stream and throughout this valley, its reliability was totally dependent on the latest flood.

Becky scampered onto the bridge as she had so many times over the years, thinking little of how its narrow structure and slick surface, often damp from spray as the waters bounced over nearby rocks, might affect others. J.C. followed immediately behind her, still not particularly encumbered by the photographer's luggage. Mr. Thompson, however, was not so agile or so fortunate. The bridge's narrow construction apparently unnerved him from the very first step. He couldn't seem to find his balance on how to walk the bridge. Halfway across, Becky watched in horror as he lurched, leaning one way then the other as his camera came close to tumbling from his shoulder.

J.C., however, wasted no time watching a tragedy unfold. He dropped the bag gently on solid ground and sprinted back across the bridge in time to relieve George Thompson of his precious load. He eased the camera from the older man's shoulder as he helped to steady him until he found his balance.

"Thank you, young man." George Thompson gasped as he caught his breath. "J.C. is it? Thank you so much, J.C. You have no idea how much misery you helped me to avert just now."

"My pleasure, sir." J.C. smiled as if this sort of venture was something he did every day. "Perhaps we should take a few minutes and rest here." He guided the photographer to a seat on a large rock under the shade of a walnut tree.

Becky stood rooted to the spot where she'd stopped after crossing the bridge. It never occurred to her that Mr. Thompson would have difficulty negotiating this bridge. It was wider than the foot bridge at the crib dam, although just barely, but it was lower too, closer to the water, and to her that made it less threatening somehow, but apparently not so for George Thompson.

"Oh, I feel terrible," she half-whispered to J.C. as he stepped away from the man seated on the rock, giving him a few moments alone to recover his dignity as well as his equilibrium. "He nearly dropped his camera in there! I never thought..."

"A person gets used to their own surroundings and doesn't think about how different they are to someone else." She wasn't sure if his soft voice was for her benefit or to avoid being overheard by the photographer.

She squinted against the sun, wrinkling her nose as she looked at him. "Come again?" was all she could think to say.

He shrugged with a grin. "My guess is you are so accustomed to tripping across the bridges and trails around here, it doesn't really occur to you that some of us are not nearly as sure-footed. It's not a bad thing. Far from it. It just means we might not always be able to keep up."

Becky turned her face away, suddenly ashamed of her earlier thoughts about J.C. She cleared her throat and asked in a husky voice, "do you think he'll be all right to continue on?"

"I imagine so." J.C. cast a glance back and then bent over to pick up a flat rock. He sent it spinning across the sparkling riffles of the stream, making several skips before it dove beneath the surface.

"All that you were telling Mr. Thompson about growing up in Panama and Cuba. That really true?"

"Es cierto," he answered in Spanish. ***"La pura verdad."***

Her eyes widened in surprise.

"It is a certainty. The pure truth." He laughed as he translated the phrases for her.

"So after all that living in such, such exotic places, you came back to a farm in Missouri?" Becky was having a difficult time trying to imagine the transition.

"Well, my parents were there and my grandparents, too. My brothers live nearby. You know, those places were truly beautiful, a little like here in that they were so green, so full of trees and life, but the really important thing about any place you feel at home isn't the place as much as the people, especially your own family."

"I can't say I ever thought about it like that," Becky answered, deep in thought.

"I met some wonderful people there. ***Buena gente,*** that's what they call them there, good people. I certainly hope to go back and visit them all again one day," he added.

After poking at the rocks around his feet, J.C. found another small flat stone which he skipped across the water, managing a half a dozen tiny splashes before it, too, disappeared. "I went to the university the last couple of years in Columbia, but my father died last year so I came home to work, and now I'm at Jefferson City, working for Senator Wiggins."

"Oh, I'm sorry about your father," Becky added quickly. "Do you like working for the senator?"

George Thompson was back on his feet, shouldering his camera once again ready to proceed. "My apologies to you both. I came down this way and took pictures of that bridge a few days ago, but I didn't get on it myself. It never occurred to me it would be difficult to cross."

"I'm sorry, too." Becky returned his apology. "I never thought about it being hard to do with your camera."

"I just didn't seem to be able to get the balance of it." The older man gave a little shake of his head with a self-deprecating laugh. "Lead on, young lady. I hope to take some extraordinary photographs before this afternoon is over, and make this all well worth our efforts."

A short while later, George Thompson had his tripod perched along the bluff trail, with the town of Brice laid out below his camera lens. He made his adjustments, taking into consideration the angle of the afternoon sunshine.

"Would you two mind to stand in a couple of these shots?" He asked after he'd taken several. "Sometimes it's an interesting change to have people in front and the landscape in the distance."

"Certainly." J.C. held out a hand to Becky as he stepped to the spot on the bluff that the photographer indicated.

She hesitated momentarily before swallowing hard and slipping her hand into his. Heights had never bothered her but something was making her heart race today and rendering her incapable of catching her breath.

"Are you all right?" His voice was soft and breathy, right next to her ear, tickling the soft hair at her neck.

"Oh, I am fine, really." She tried to sound more confident than she felt and was thankful neither of them could see her wobbling knees beneath her long skirt.

Mr. Thompson took his photographs as the afternoon passed by like a sun-dappled dream, all wrapped up in the warmth of a soft Ozark breeze caressing her cheek.

They were near the Brice Inn on their return trek when Becky spied her father approaching as he rode Betsy down through the valley. As always, she was happy to see him, although he usually made it home long before now. She waved and he reined Betsy to a stop right in front of them. She eagerly introduced him to her companions, who took the opportunity to ease their photographic burdens gently to a small patch of grassy ground in front of the inn.

"This is my father, Zeb Darling." She finished her introductions. "I was showing Mr. Thompson the best places for a photograph up along the bluff," Becky explained. "And Mr. Shine came along to see for himself. He and his boss, the senator, are here from Jefferson City."

"Yes, I'm aware of their mission here." Her father's serious gray eyes settled on her, a new concern she couldn't quite explain drawing his forehead into a slight frown.

Becky, always proud of her father, found herself silently praying for the first time in her life that he wouldn't say anything that would embarrass her.

"Gentlemen." Zeb Darling managed to remain cordial despite his personal feelings. "Enjoying the valley, are you?"

"Oh, yes, it's quite a place," the older man spoke first. "I'd seen it in photographs before but they don't do it justice. I hope mine will, but it is a place that speaks for itself, the kind that you really have to experience rather than to just see on paper."

"That describes it well," J.C. agreed heartily. "'Tis a beautiful location, Mr. Darling. You must feel very blessed to live here throughout the year, rather than to simply visit like the rest of us."

"Well, yes." Zebulon Darling's surprise at the younger man's words could be seen on his face. "Yes, I do. It's not something that one takes for granted, that's for certain."

"I can appreciate that," J.C. continued. "It's been a wonderful excursion today." He turned back to Becky and shook Mr. Thompson's hand. "I'll leave your bag for you on the porch there. I'd best be catching up to the senator and find out if he has anything that requires my assistance. Mr. Darling, it was a pleasure to meet you." He tipped his cap to the man still seated on his horse, snatched up the bag which he deposited on the inn's wooden porch and disappeared inside.

"Guess I'll be seeing you at home soon, young lady." Her father in turn bid them farewell and nudged Betsy with his heels, guiding her in the direction of the spring. It was then that Becky first caught sight of papers and a hammer sticking out of the back of one of his saddlebags.

Becky tried silently to determine why she felt so odd, a little confused and yet strangely more confident about life in general than she ever had. She tried to shake off the strange sensation and pay attention to what Mr. Thompson was saying as they went up the steps.

"That J.C. Shine is quite an impressive young man," he spoke as if to himself but Becky took in every word. "He's seen more than a bit of the world, is most considerate and helpful and has a real appreciation of the beauty of this place. A great many his age only seem to be interested in how fast these new cars will go and in where the nearest speakeasy is located. Yes," he shook his head slightly as he slung his bag onto his shoulder and picked up his camera. "He's quite an impressive young man."

Chapter 6

"I didn't realize playing tour guide was one of your duties down there at the Brice Inn." Her father had maintained his silence during most of the dinner her mother had made that evening, chicken and dumplings and fresh poke salad, that Becky had gathered along the roadside on her way home that day. But now Ma's normally delicious flat noodle dumplings lay like one big lump in her stomach.

"I thought you were down there to help with cleaning and dishes and such," he added.

Becky tried to determine where his objections were going next. "Pa, I just do whatever Miz Josie says she needs. Most of the time it's like you said, cleaning, dishes, laundry. Today she was the one who suggested I take Mr. Thompson, the photographer, up on the bluff so he could get a better view of the town."

"Uh-huh, and that senator's aide. Did he get a good view, too?"

Becky's eyes narrowed as she looked up from her dinner bowl. "He asked if he could come along and Miz Josie said that would be fine." She tried to keep her voice steady and not let her mounting irritation show. "As it turns out, he saved Mr. Thompson's camera when he almost dropped it in the stream. That photographer man got sort of unbalanced on the low bridge and J.C., he just reached out and pulled him back."

"Well, you just make sure he's not reaching out for anything else while you're squiring him around, you hear?"

"Zebulon!" His wife's voice cut through the tension between father and daughter.

"You weren't there today, Hannah! You didn't see the way he was...he was..."

"He was what, Pa?" Becky's indignation was immediate. "He didn't do nothing. He didn't say nothing that was even a little bit out of line!"

"He didn't do anything." Her mother corrected her under her breath.

"He didn't!" Becky whirled with a sharp edge to her voice.

"Why are you defending him with such fervor?" Zeb countered. "You sure didn't seem to be unhappy with the attention that was coming your way, from what I could see. If he means nothing to you..." He left the sentence unfinished.

"I didn't say he did. I didn't say he didn't," she answered back, standing up as she spoke.

"Where are you going?"

"Anywhere. I don't know. I don't care to sit here and be accused of nothing. I can't believe this. What is it you think?"

"I think I don't like flatlanders coming in here and visiting with my daughter without my knowledge or permission. I think you're getting mighty big and mighty sassy with your father over nothing!" Zeb was also on his feet.

"Flatlanders! Pa, you were a flatlander once and you came here and that's how you met Ma—"

"Stop it, both of you!" Hannah spoke without standing but her raised voice was enough. Benji's bright eyes continued to flit back and forth, taking in the verbal sparring match without saying a word.

Becky bit her lip, tears of anger making her eyes smart.

"Is that what this is about? You taking up with that flatlander against your own pa?"

"You have no idea, no idea at all!" With that Becky knocked her chair over backwards as she spun on her heel. She tripped over the saddlebag her father had dropped by the door. The papers she'd seen earlier on the back of Betsy cascaded across the floor. She knelt down to retrieve them and then straightened slowly as the realization dawned.

Meeting at the Confluence Bridge, 6 pm Thursday

Why We Don't Need A Park in this Valley

The small handmade posters only added fuel to the fire already burning inside her. She threw them on top of the saddle bags, instead of tucking them back inside and walked out the door, slamming it behind her.

"Now look at what you both have done!" Hannah stood up and moved the heavy iron pot off the table and back onto the stove. "I make my best chicken and dumplings, thinking it is one of the few things that sounded real comfortin' about now, steamy and tasty, and you two get into a shouting match about some outsider neither one of you knows!"

"How do you know she doesn't know him?" Zeb grumbled as he poked at the uneaten dumplings still in front of him.

"Because she hasn't said more than ten words about him to me, that's how. If'n he was all that important to her, she would have said so by now. You and your suspicions could be pushing our girl right out the door before her time has even come!"

"Hannah, I'm sorry." Zebulon Darling looked as miserable as he felt as he mopped his forehead in exasperation with a red handkerchief he pulled from his back pocket. "It just scares me, the idea of some handsome young feller from who knows where, taking off with her or worse yet, convincing her to go."

"Then tell her that, straight from the heart." His wife's voice gentled as if she were talking to a small child. "Don't be fussing at her about things she can't control, like what he does or says or even how she feels. She is a woman now, Zeb, whether you like it or not."

"I know, I know," he mumbled as much to himself as to his wife.

"It's like you've forgotten how much she loves you, loves us and all the things you've taught her over the years. Show some faith in her. That's what's hurting her right now as much as anything."

Zeb didn't respond, keeping his eyes fastened on the uneaten food in front of him, both elbows now resting on the table.

"If you handle this badly, you could have more to do with driving her away than any young man sniffing around our door."

"I know, I know," he repeated.

"Who's sniffing at the door?" Benji looked suspiciously at the entrance of their home, where his sister had made her noisy exit.

"Never you mind, listening to other people's conversations," his mother reprimanded him, not unkindly and patted him on the shoulder. "Eat your dinner. I daresay you're the only who still has any appetite left."

Outside, Becky hiked swiftly away from the house in her anger but slowed as she approached the spring. If there was anyone around she didn't want to be answering questions about why she was upset. Miz Josie was right about one thing. Gossip was a favorite activity here in the valley and she didn't care to be the subject of it.

She slipped along the spring trail, hoping the sheltering white arms of the sycamores there would help her feel better. Her town friend, Georgia, once remarked, "I'd be afraid living out there in the woods, the way you do. You live in the forest, just like Hansel and Gretel. All those trees so close up, surrounding your house, they seem scary to me."

Becky had laughed out loud when she said that. She could not imagine trying to explain how comforting and protective she found the trees to be. It was as if they reached out and formed a shelter against all dangers, real or imagined, the few here in the valley and the many that waited in the outside world. Could they make her feel better about the threats that even came from her own household, she wondered, as she meandered down the stony foot trail that ran along the water's edge. She watched as a bluebird zipped by on its way to its nest, to raise a new brood of baby birds at this time of year.

It wasn't the sycamores or the bluebirds that brought her up short however, a few steps further along the well-worn trail. Instead, a movement down by the water caught her eye in the early evening's slanting sunlight. A man with a creel basket hanging from his side cast a line out across the water. Becky took a step back and settled herself on a large moss-covered rock alongside the trail.

She had seen others fly fishing along the spring branch, of course, and she had more than once thought it was a skill she would like to learn some day. When she went fishing it was to a great extent for the sheer joy of it, but it was also to catch fish, edible fish, one more way she and her parents labored to put food on the family table. This was different. There was a beauty, a majesty to fly fishing, she could not begin to explain or even describe. She watched, mesmerized, as the line floated out again, an extension of the man's arm as he held the finely-crafted fly rod. Again and again, the line flew, floated and then landed with no sound at all, delicately dropping the feathered fly onto the surface of the water. Then it whipped back in response to the fisherman's bidding. After several minutes, she looked past the immediate actions of the man standing in hip boots in the shallow waters. His face was more hidden than not under the cloth hat that he wore but after a few more moments she was convinced of his identity.

J.C. Shine cast out his line again, but as he started once more to strip the line with his free hand, he raised his rod tip sharply instead. A large shining rainbow trout leapt out of the waters and twisted high in the early evening sunshine.

"Oh!" Becky let out only the single word but it was enough to snap the fisherman's eyes off of his quarry and send them searching the bank for its source.

The shift of his attention made for a small momentary slack in the line as the rod tip dipped. That was all the graceful arching fish needed to leap free and swim away to be caught another day.

"I'm so sorry!" Becky gasped as she realized what had happened.

"What are you doing in there?" J.C. pulled in his line as he walked across the shallow waters of the stream in her direction. "How long have you been sitting there?"

"Oh, I just stopped to—" Becky realized she had no good explanation for why she was there. She hopped to her feet as he drew closer.

She dropped her eyes for a split second and then shifted the conversation. "You look like quite the expert fisherman there."

"Oh, no." He grinned as he stepped up on the bank in front of her. "My oldest brother went to Colorado last summer on a business trip and I got to tag along. We went trout fishing several times and he bought all the equipment. Most of this is his. Joe let me borrow it when I told him I was coming down here with the senator. The hat is the only thing that is mine." He reached up and pulled the light brown canvas hat from his head, letting his straight blond hair fall down across his forehead.

"Well, you were doing a very fine job of fishing, borrowed equipment or not," Becky observed with honest admiration. "I'm sorry if I distracted you and made you lose your trout."

"Oh, it's not a problem." He grinned. "It just means I'll have to catch another. That is the joy of it, isn't it? Catching one after another, whether you get to keep them or not."

"Oh, I don't know." Becky hedged. "I try to keep the ones I catch, trout, catfish, bass, goggle-eye, all of them."

"Oh, I see. You are a real fisherman or, I should say, fisherwoman. You keep them all."

"Yes, I keep them all, but I think you are the real fisherman, with the fine way you throw that line."

"You don't fly fish?"

"No." She shook her head and smiled demurely. "I would like to someday, perhaps, but not right now."

"Really? But you live here."

"Yes, I live here," she answered evenly, "but that doesn't leave a lot of time for the likes of trout fishing."

"It doesn't? Now I'm confused."

She sighed, trying to figure out the best way to explain the situation. "Do you remember earlier today when you told my pa he must feel really blessed to live here?" Becky reached down and pulled a bit of purple and green wood sorrel from near the large rock where she had been seated.

He nodded. "I do."

"Well, it's funny you should say that because Pa says that all the time. He says that we are blessed to live here, but that while the Ozarks is a beautiful place to live, it ain't an easy place to make a living." She looked at the wood sorrel in her hand, wiped it on her dress and then popped it into her mouth.

J.C. wrinkled up his nose without comment.

"He says we work hard here to make what little we do because the real payoff is living in such a beautiful place. Does that make sense?"

"It does."

"Well, it also means we spend a goodly portion of our time working or making things or even fishing, for food, not for sport. Beautiful as it is, your fly fishing is more for sport than for the fish you take home at the end of the day."

The man before her looked down at his boots and nodded his head. "Fair enough, Miss Becky. Fair enough." They stood in awkward silence for a moment before he added, "and thank you."

"For what?"

"That could prove to be valuable information tomorrow."

"And what is tomorrow?"

He sighed as he began to pull in his line and wind it onto the reel. "I checked in with the senator when we first got back today, but he said he really did not need anything until later this evening. Tomorrow we'll begin meeting with persons who live here, who, like you said, have to work hard every day to put food on the table. And in Lebanon, we'll be meeting with business men from the Chamber of Commerce amongst others. I understand there are some business people who are most anxious to have a state park here. Did you know it will be the first Missouri state park if all goes as planned? That's quite an honor."

"I had no idea," she admitted, shaking her head. "You know," she continued, trying to think of the best way to broach the subject, "there are some folks who don't want the park here. Not bad people, you know, just folks who are confused maybe as to what it will all mean, how it will all go."

"Oh, I'm sure that's true." He finished packing up his gear. "And we certainly want to allay their fears. That's another part of why we're here, to try to reassure folks that this will be a good thing in the long run. Change is always hard for people." He shook his head slightly as he smiled. "I understand that better than most, I guess."

He stood up straight and she noticed again how tall he was, not unlike one of her beloved sycamore trees, tall and straight and strong.

"I have to catch up with the senator for supper now and we have some papers to go over before tomorrow."

Becky edged down the path in the direction of her home. "Well, then good luck to you tomorrow. I hope it all goes well." As she walked away, she glanced about, with a fleeting thought of how much angrier her father would be right now to once again find her talking so freely with this outsider. For her part, however, she felt oddly comforted by her chance encounter with J.C. Shine and his calm approach to what were certainly threatening storms in her life.

The next day was a quiet, uneventful day at the inn, for which Becky was thankful as it gave her time to catch up on cleaning and changing out rooms. Mr. Thompson moved on to his next assignment, thanking Josie and Becky profusely before packing his things into an older Model A Ford and heading back towards Lebanon.

The senator and J.C. spent the entire day in meetings with men in Lebanon. Mr. Taylor was outside most of the day. Becky caught glimpses of him strolling alongside the spring branch, stopping by the grist mill, and just sort of wandering about. He didn't come in for a meal at noon but he was ready for something much later in the day.

Becky told him Miz Josie had made fried chicken for dinner and she offered to warm it up for him. He insisted cold fried chicken would be fine. Becky did take the time to make potato pancakes, fried with crispy edges all around, from some of the left over mashed potatoes. She served it all with warmed gravy and biscuits on the side.

"It looks wonderful," he exclaimed as she laid out the late afternoon meal for him. He was the only one in the parlor at this time of day.

"Likewise, this has been such a wonderful couple of days," he mused as he ate. Becky took the opportunity to pour herself a glass of cold tea and sit down at the far table for a few moments.

"I didn't see you fishing," Becky ventured. "What have you done?"

"Rested, my girl, simply rested, and that has been a godsend."

Becky wasn't sure what to say.

"I run a company in St. Louis with my brothers, John and Thomas, Taylor Brothers Manufacturing, and sometimes the stress of that sort of thing...." He stopped to take a bite.

"So many people think that running a family business is the way to do things, but I can tell you, there is something to be said for the business in which no one is related and everyone simply comes to work and goes home again, leaving their family worries out of it altogether!"

"I don't really know." Becky tried to be polite although she had no idea what the man was talking about. "I've only worked for Miz Josie here at the hotel and that has been very nice."

"You're a smart girl." Lee Taylor nodded in her direction as he put down his fork and attacked the fried chicken with both hands. "Keep it that way. Work for someone who is not your relative. Working for and with my brothers has about driven me to strong drink. I had to travel to Springfield on business anyway, but truly the couple of days I've spent here with you fine people has been a tonic to my soul, and I thank you."

"Well, you are very welcome." Becky finished her tea and stood up to take her empty glass back to the kitchen. "Would you like some dessert? I believe Miz Josie made pies today, gooseberry and cherry and there is still cake too."

"Oh, gooseberry pie. Now that would be a treat."

Becky brought it to him on a china saucer as Josie came in from the back.

"I was just telling this young lady how much I've enjoyed my time here," Lee Taylor told her. "I am only sorry I have to go on to Springfield first thing tomorrow."

"Well, we're sorry, too." Josie plopped down at her customary table. Becky took one look at the weary proprietress of the hotel and immediately fetched another glass of tea.

"Would you like anything else?" she asked.

"No, sweetie, I'm fine. Thank you for this though. I could certainly use it about now. I'm glad we've been able to offer you a little rest and relaxation while you were here and we certainly hope you'll come back."

"I would like that very much," he answered as he wiped his hands on his napkin. Becky set the gooseberry pie, tart and green, before him. "That looks delicious," he said. "Just like my mother used to make. First though, I just thought of something."

He got up from the table and hurried out the front door. Becky and Josie exchanged puzzled looks, which only deepened when he returned a few moments later with a large glass jar, with a hand-crank piece of machinery attached to the top.

"Miz Josie, I would be most honored if you would allow me to leave this with you. This is one of our newest models, called the Reliable butter churn. My brothers and I make these at our company. We are in negotiations right now with the Dazey people, perhaps you've heard of them? I think when all is said and done, we will probably end up turning this part of the manufacturing over to them, but in the meantime, I would really like to make a gift of one of these to you if that would be acceptable."

"Oh, Miz Josie," Becky immediately gushed. "It's beautiful! Look at it! With a clear glass jar and all, lots better than the crock one we use. Why, you can see the butter right there in front of your eyes while you're making it!"

"Yes, that is rather what we thought." Lee Taylor sat back down to his pie, enjoying the women's reaction to his butter churn.

"Why, Mr. Taylor, I don't quite know what to say." It was a rare man that caught Josie Smith at a loss for words. "Except of course, thank you very much for your kindness."

"Oh no, thank you, dear lady. My brothers are the mechanical geniuses that manage to keep inventing new ways to do things. It is my job to keep the company books and try to keep them on the straight and narrow. It can be a stressful business, I don't mind telling you. These days here with you have meant so much. It is my pleasure."

After he had left the parlor, Josie looked at Becky again. "Well, you just never know." She shook her head. "I just came from talking with Sherman next door. One thing I have to agree on, working with your brother can certainly be a trial. He is all wound up about this park thing again, of course, now that the senator is here."

"Oh, I'm so tired of hearing about it, Miz Josie," Becky spoke more honestly than she had intended. "Oh, I'm sorry, ma'am."

"It's all right, Becky. I imagine that you are worn slick with it by now, knowing how your pa feels about it and all. That's part of what's got Sherman all stirred up. I guess those boys that are against a park wanted to hold their meeting at the store or over at the church and Sherman said no, so they got mad and have called a meeting for tomorrow night down at the confluence. As I understand it, they borried a tent used for tent revivals and they're putting it up down there. That'll at least give them a place to cuss and discuss 'til they get tired." She chuckled at her own little joke despite her fatigue.

"Oh, Miz Josie, I am so sorry," Becky repeated. "I know my pa is being so difficult about this whole thing. I think he's just scared. He thinks this means the end of the town of Brice and the end of the post office and his job. And, well, you can understand that, can't you?"

"Of course, Becky, I do understand." She sighed. "A man has to support his family the best way he can and heaven knows, your pa is doing a good job of it. I wish I could tell him, flat out, he's got nothing to worry about, but I don't rightly know that's true. Maybe the senator will have some answers for them. Part of what had Sherman so upset is that the senator told him this morning that he intends to go to that meeting down at the river, so now Sherman is thinking he shouldn't have refused them a proper place for it. He says it ain't fittin' for a senator to have to go stand around on a river bank to conduct business. He got even madder when I laughed at him and said it was his own doing, nobody else's. I guess I should have been more sympathetic, but nobody can gum up the works on something like this faster than a bunch of men, I swear!"

"Miz Josie," Becky giggled.

"Well, it's true. They talk and they talk and they talk. Truth be told, they can talk an issue to death in the time it takes a woman to get the job done, whatever it might be. Good thing our children don't have to depend on their fathers to feed them, put them to bed and change their britches. All that talk won't help a lick with any of that!"

Becky shook her head with a grin as she stood up from the table. "Miz Josie, I best be headed towards home. It's getting late."

"Yes, it is, and I'm sure you've got chores waiting for you yet when you get there."

As she reached the front door, Josie called her back. "About that butter churn. Mr. Taylor said he would be leaving in the morning, so we'd best leave it here until he's on his way, but after that, I expect you need to take it on up the road to your house. You and yours are the ones making the butter we use around here and I certainly don't want to go back to it. So after tomorrow you take it along and see what you think of the Taylor brothers' newest invention and let me know, will you?"

"Oh I will, Miz Josie!" Becky's eyes shown at the thought of it. "You can be sure I will!"

Chapter 7

It was a clear and lovely Ozark evening with a gentle breeze and the sun reflecting lazily off the spring branch waters as they mingled with those of the Niangua River. A large crowd had gathered at the site of a large canvas tent next to the confluence. A popular place for picnics and Sunday afternoon outings, today's gathering held the potential for deliverance or disaster.

Becky had spent the day in agony, her stomach reeling with anticipation and dread as to what might actually develop out of this meeting her father and others had called. One part of her fretted that it said much about the community as a whole that local leaders had refused them a building in which to hold it. On the other hand, the senator himself had expressed his intention to attend, so that must lend more than a touch of legitimacy to the entire undertaking. All day long, her fears swirled within her as she tried to concentrate on dishes, laundry and the like. Although her hands were busy, her mind was always on the business at hand, and now the hour that she had been dreading had finally arrived.

At the end of her day at the inn, she carried the new glass butter churn home as per her boss's instructions. She hadn't mentioned it the day before, wanting instead to simply present it to her mother.

"What is this?" Hannah Darling looked up from the ham sandwiches she was putting together when Becky walked in.

"This is a brand new butter churn that Mr. Taylor, one of the hotel guests, gave to Miz Josie when he left," she announced proudly.

"Well, I can see that," her mother answered, "but what is it doing here?"

"Miz Josie says we make the butter for her now, so she thought we could try it out and tell her what we think of it. She said she has no desire to go back to making her own butter."

"But she can't just give a thing like that away." Her mother put both hands around the square glass jar and then began to turn the smooth crank that glided through its motions with little resistance as compared to other churns she'd used.

"She's just loaning it to us, I'm sure," Becky said. "For as long as we make the butter, she said she was happy for us to have it here."

Her mother snorted but smiled in approval all the while. "Well, I don't suppose we better complain about that. You and Benji will have to see how you like it.

"Come on now. I'm going to finish up these sandwiches and I need you to go out and bring in a bit more wood for the stove. I'll need it tomorrow for baking bread. Then we have to go meet your father—"

"Meet Pa? Where?"

"At that meeting at the confluence, of course."

"But Ma, we're all going?"

"Well, of course, we're all going. I expect about everybody in Brice, the whole of the Bennett Spring valley as well as some from outside will be there. What did you think?"

"I...I don't know," Becky stammered. "I just never thought you..." Her voice trailed off because she really did not have an answer to the question.

"Look, Becky." Her mother stopped working to look her daughter square in the eye. "I know this has been hard on you and for that I am truly sorry. I don't say I agree completely with your father in all of this but he has a right like anyone else to express his opinion. He does have a real concern for his job and how we will live here if they do make this park, so I understand why he's doing this."

She went back to slicing bread, with a vengeance this time. "I think it was ridiculous of those men on the church board to refuse them the use of the church for their meeting, but that's truly water under the bridge now. Nobody could tell them they couldn't meet out in the open air and that's what they've decided to do. I'm just glad it ain't raining today. That might have been a sign from the good Lord as to what He thinks of this whole thing." A little laugh escaped her.

"The truth is, don't any of us know how this is all going to turn out and it may be none of us has a real say in it, but regardless, I think we need to be there as a family. We need to be united and let your father know that we believe in him, no matter what happens. We are truly the reason he is doing this. Do you understand that?"

Becky nodded. "Yes ma'am." She went outside to find the chopping ax. Hannah Darling was not the speech maker in the family. She leaned most often towards pithy remarks and short parables, so when she took the time to say more than a few words on any subject, Becky knew it was of the utmost importance. She took the ax to the piece of wood in front of her and split it right down the middle. Then she grabbed up the pieces and did the same again. She thought about the new butter churn. Machines to do everything, that's what it seemed like the world was coming to, cars and newer and better butter churns. She was certainly ready for somebody to invent a machine that would split wood for her, she thought, as she dropped the ax down through another small log, making pieces small enough to be fed easily into the wood cook stove. She repeated the process a half dozen times and then quickly gathered up what she had and took it inside to drop in the box beside the stove.

She walked with her mother and Benji down the road along the spring branch towards the confluence, dreading what might be coming. By the time they arrived, the tent was filled and people were standing around on all sides of the tent. The flaps had been rolled up and tied out of the way, making it into a large canvas awning to better accommodate the growing crowd.

"Thank you, thank you for coming." It was her father's voice, calling the group to order. "We invited you all here tonight to talk about this here proposal to make a park out of our town. I realize the details are still up in the air, but the long and the short of it is that…"

His voice droned on but Becky found she was unable to concentrate on his words. The crowd listened intently and then broke into spontaneous applause a couple of times.

"Excuse me, Mr. Chairman. Mr. Darling, is it?" Becky could see the rotund Senator Wiggins step up close to where her father was and hold out his hand. "We haven't met yet, sir, but perhaps, if you will allow me, I can save everyone, including yourself, a great deal of time and trouble. I know this is your meeting and I certainly don't wish to step on any toes, but if I can lay out some of the plans that are being pulled together as we speak in Jefferson City, I'm sure I can alleviate many of the fears and rumors that you have heard…"

With that opening, Senator Wiggins began to present the legislative plans to establish Missouri's first state park. He went on to explain how Lebanon Chamber of Commerce leaders had actually asked those in charge in Jefferson City to consider the area as the possible site for this "great honor."

Becky watched as her mother found a seat for herself and Benji off to the far side on some large rocks. Hannah handed Benji one of the ham sandwiches and the two of them sat there, munching as they listened. Holding their own picnic, Becky thought, in the midst of what she had feared would be total chaos.

At the back of the crowd, Becky saw another familiar face, Buster Kendrix. The tall, rawboned man wearing nothing but a pair of overalls and a smashed down, worn out hat always looked like "he was just waking up" as her father had once put it. He stood with his arms folded across his chest, watching and listening, a lit cigarette dangling from his lower lip.

Becky slid up behind him on his right side. "Where's my brother?" was all she said.

"Well, Miss Becky Darling," he drawled, as he straightened up and smiled at her.

"You heard me." Becky looked a hole right through him. "Where's my brother?"

"Hm, you're in a right friendly mood now, aren't you?"

"You know why I'm not."

"Yes, well, Jake is busy tonight is all." He let his gaze travel back to the front of the crowd, as if he was actually interested in what was being said, but Becky didn't believe it.

"You mean you've got him busy," she whispered as she glanced around at those standing nearby.

Buster cleared his throat and looked down at her with a grin, paying little attention to her outrage. "What he said was he wasn't much interested in all this park talk, but I told him I wanted to hear what the folks involved had to say. So he said he'd stay on the hill tonight and I decided to come on down and see what's up."

"I know what you left him doing up there," she whispered again, "and I'm telling you this, Buster. If anything happens to my brother, I'm going to be on you like stink on a polecat! You better be looking out for him or you'll have more to deal with than you know what to do with."

The big man chuckled as he crossed his arms again, resuming his original stance. "I'll be sure to keep that in mind, Sis," was all he said, and went back to listening to the last of the senator's remarks.

"Therefore, we'll be conducting these interviews across the course of the next few days. I'd encourage any of you who have serious concerns about this new state park to get with my aide here, young Mr. J.C. Shine. Hold up your hand, J.C., so they can see who you are."

The senator's aide obliged his boss and gave a little wave to the crowd.

"Come by and schedule a time to talk with me about this. Now I don't want to take up everyone's time here this evening, but I did want to take the opportunity to let you know that we are seriously interested in hearing everyone's opinion about this new venture." And with that, the tension that Becky had felt building all day long began to melt away. A few asked questions, including her father, who wanted to know what might happen to those who would lose their jobs as a result of this proposed park.

"The truth is that such a park would create as many jobs as it might eventually wipe out, probably more." The senator spoke again. "We have not determined exactly who or what but nothing is going to happen overnight. This will be a slow process, I assure you. As some jobs go, others will come in. The grist mill, of course, will continue to operate, despite what some of you have heard, and, uh…" He hesitated and another questioner called out.

"What about the saw mill?"

"Well, now the saw mill might be another question. Obviously we wouldn't have a saw mill operating in the middle of a state park, but that doesn't mean it can't be relocated somewhere outside the confines of the park or that a new one couldn't be started elsewhere. Again, I feel certain that while those jobs will be directly affected by this proposal, there will be jobs created by the coming of the park and…." He droned on and in short order, it was over. All her worries, all her anxieties had been for naught.

"Hey folks!" Josie Bennett Smith's was the next voice she heard coming from the front, although she couldn't see the short-statured lady who was speaking. "Since everyone is out and about already, I'd like to invite you to come by the Brice Inn yet this evening. We've got some fresh pie and cake and coffee available and it's a shame to waste a perfectly good evening. Now that the business is over, let's enjoy a little time together as neighbors. I'm headed up the road right now and I do hope you'll stop by."

Becky glanced around and saw that her mother and father and little brother were all standing to one side up at the front, not far from where the senator was shaking hands with everyone and accepting their thanks-for-coming accolades. J.C. was also busy, talking with folks and making notes in a notebook. No doubt, the senator's calendar, she thought. As she moved in that general direction, J.C. clapped the notebook shut and thanked the man standing at his side. He moved towards her with an unexpected urgency and gently took her elbow, guiding her outside the tent and away from the others.

"I'm so glad to see you," he said, surprising her again. "I have a question for you and I hope..." He easily looked over the tops of the heads of most of the people in the dispersing crowd. "There!" he said, trying to keep his voice low despite his apparent excitement. "That woman there. She has kind of red hair with gray in it. Who is she?"

Becky couldn't imagine what his interest could be, but she followed his line of sight, watching him as much as the woman he was attempting to point out without actually raising his hand.

"That's Mrs. Stone, Gertrude Stone, the saw mill manager's wife," she said. "Why?"

"Gertrude," he said, as he let the name roll off his tongue. "Of course. Gertrude."

"They call her Trudy, the other ladies do. To be honest, I try not to call her anything at all. She's not very nice much of the time." Becky cast a furtive glance over her shoulder but her parents were involved in a lively conversation with another couple, so at least for the time being, she figured she was out of harm's way.

"How do you mean?" He turned his attention back to her, seeming to forget about the departing Mrs. Stone.

"Oh, you know, she is just cantankerous, always cranky. She doesn't talk very nice about Miz Josie for one thing, so I don't like her much and I do my best to stay away from her. How do you know her?"

"Oh, I don't." He turned to shake hands with another one of the departing men. "She just caught my eye is all, that red hair, I suppose."

"And is that what it takes to catch your eye? Red hair?" Becky could not believe she was saying the words as fast as they popped out. She hated when girls talked like that, like her friend, Georgia, anytime there were boys around. What was she thinking?

"No." He laughed out loud. "I was just surprised by it, I guess, and it had me wondering. It's really not important."

The lie was not convincing, Becky thought as she watched his nostrils flare slightly as he spoke. If he was going to be a politician like his boss, he'd have to learn to do a better job than that of not telling the truth.

"Well, I'd best get down to the inn and see if Miz Josie needs any help. If even half these folks accept her invitation, the place will be full in short order."

"We'll be along pretty quickly, too, I imagine," J.C. replied. "I'll see you there."

Becky nodded without saying any more. She found her mother and informed her of where she was going and hurried on to catch up to Miz Josie down the road.

As she predicted, the place was packed but it was such a happy crowd that Becky was more thrilled than ever to be working there. She put out plates of pie and cake until she ran out of plates and had to hurriedly go back to the kitchen to wash a few to keep up with the demand. Miz Josie had been smart enough to get all three coffee pots going on the stove before she left for the meeting, and for that Becky was thankful as she poured coffee, tea and just plain sparkling spring water to dozens of guests.

She heard Miz Josie's voice cry out at one point. "Red, where's that fiddle of yours?"

"Over in the back of Jonathan Stone's automobile, Miz Josie," he answered. "We took it with us to a dance last Saturday night in Buffalo." The next thing Becky heard were the sweet violin melodies that nobody could play like Red Flaherty. Becky had heard him tell people before he couldn't read a note of music but it didn't matter. He could hear a song, any song, and then make his fiddle sing it and everyone in the valley loved listening to the way Red played. Familiar dance rhythms, soothing lullabies, even the sweet strains of spirituals and gospel tunes filled the night air adding to the festive mood.

Her parents didn't stop by the inn, and for that Becky was sorry. It was such a party and she would have loved for her mother to have the chance to enjoy it too, but then she realized, maybe her father was unhappy with how it had all gone tonight. If he was in a foul mood as a result, she was glad he had passed on by on their way home. Still, it was a shame, but maybe, just maybe it meant things would be more peaceful from now on.

She didn't have much time to think about it as she continued to help Miz Josie play hostess to her many guests, and then suddenly, it was over. The last of the visitors bid them farewell, although a couple of the men remained outside, talking to the senator. They stood close by his car and Becky caught the scent of cigar smoke on the night air. The inn was hushed and Becky realized, for the first time all evening, how tired she really was.

"Miz Josie," she spoke when the older woman came through the kitchen doorway as Becky finished up the last of the dishes. "I think I'll be going home now so I can be back in the morning on time."

"Yes, it is high time you headed that way. I sure do appreciate your help tonight, Becky. You tell your mama and your pa, thank you, too, will you? For letting you stay so late."

"I will." Becky nodded as she dried her hands on her apron and then slipped it off over her head and onto the peg near the door. "Do you need anything else before I go?"

"No, no, child. I'm fine, really." She walked back out into the parlor area and Becky followed.

"Oh, you might tell your mama when you get a chance. If she has any cabbages in her garden that she's ready to part with, I've had quite the hankering for a batch of cole slaw lately. If she has cabbages to sell, I'd be interested."

Becky grinned. "I'll tell her. I'm sure we've got some ready."

She started for the door just as J.C. came in from outside. "Going home now?" He raised an eyebrow in her direction.

"Yes, I am."

"May I drive you?" he offered.

"Oh, no." A smile of trepidation crossed her face. "It's not that far. I always walk."

She thought with more than a twinge of guilt about how quickly she had accepted a ride from her brother a few weeks ago across the same distance. But this was different, totally different.

"Well then, may I walk with you?"

Becky looked back at Miz Josie for help, but she didn't get the kind of aid she was expecting.

"Of course, you can." Josie encouraged. "Never hurts to have an escort after dark, even here at Bennett Spring."

Becky turned back, realizing she was on her own. "Ma always says there ain't nothing out there in the dark that wasn't there in the daylight, so it's foolishness that some people make such a fuss about going outside after dark."

"And do you believe that?" J.C. asked as he opened the door for her and followed her out.

Josie Smith shook her head as she watched them go. What that girl didn't understand about catching a man would fill volumes. Ask her to catch fish and she was all business, but this other was a whole new world to her.

Becky stepped off the porch, turning towards the gate. "It makes sense, I suppose," Becky answered evenly. "I know there are lots of people who are afraid of the dark but I don't guess I've ever been one of them."

"Due in part, I'm sure, to your mother's sensible raising," J.C. countered.

Becky shrugged. "Maybe. I guess it's also because we've always lived out here in the woods, in the forest as my friend, Georgia, likes to say. She lives in town and she's used to street lights, electric lights, gas lights, all kind of lights. We don't have that so much out here so I guess we've just gotten accustomed to it. I mean Miz Josie she has electric lights here at the inn and running water, too, but country folks, we are used to making do and I can't say we spend a lot of time thinking about it."

"I suppose that's true," J.C. answered. They walked along in silence, the soft dust muffling even their footsteps. For the first time, all night, Becky noticed a full moon hung above them, bathing the area in pale, almost blue, light.

"Don't you love the full moon?" she asked, as she stopped and cast her eyes skyward. "Look here." She ducked under the nearby trees and emerged quickly on the other side at the water's edge. "See how lovely the moon is on the spring branch at night?"

"It is incredible," J.C. replied, looking first at the water and then at his equally lovely companion, her face bathed in moonlight and the afterglow of the excitement of the whole evening.

"So tonight went better than you expected?"

"Oh yes!" Becky let out a sigh of relief. "You have no idea how worried I was."

As they came over the rise not far from the crib dam, a deer stamped and snorted and scampered across the way in front of them, white tail bobbing jauntily in the moonlight.

"Do you know how special that was?" Becky cried out as she reached for his arm. "I can't remember the last time I saw a deer down here. They've about hunted them all out of this valley. They are so light on their feet. Makes me wish I could run like that!"

J.C. couldn't help but notice the excitement in her eyes despite her fatigue. "You looked pretty light on your feet the other day on that hiking trail," he said softly. "So tell me what had you so worried about this meeting tonight?"

"Just about everything!" Becky launched into a litany of unrequited dreads, from her father's attitude to the response of the rest of the community. "I just knew not only was Pa going to throw some kind of fit up there, I figured nobody in the valley would even be talking to us by the time it was all said and done."

J.C.'s laughter exploded at her description of impending disaster. "You really were in a full panic about this?" Another step and their conversation was interrupted by a blood-curdling shriek and a sudden flapping noise that filled the air. Coming from the stream's edge, now hidden in the darkness, it made them both jump. "What in the name of holiness was that?" he gasped.

Now it was Becky's turn to laugh. "It's just a great blue," she chortled, taking in his frightened expression. "A great blue heron. Maybe Ma's right. They are all around in the daytime too, but you don't notice them much. But when they give a screech at night catching up fish, when you're walking along the water's edge, it is kinda startlin'."

"Kinda startlin'? Those old boys out there talking to the senator tonight were telling stories about all kinds of things, including 'haints', as one of them called ghosts. With sounds like that, I'm not surprised. It wouldn't take much to convince a person there was some tortured soul out there, lost forever in the river." He shook his head with a grin on his face, but Becky noticed he edged ever so slightly closer to the road, away from the stream bank and closer to her as they walked.

At the spring, they stopped to watch the dark waters well up, sparkling silver, yet silent, in the moonlight. "Isn't it beautiful?"

"Yes, it is," he agreed. "You do live in a beautiful place, Becky Darling."

"I always feel like this is some sort of a heart, like a heart beating and all the water flowing, it's like the life of this place," Becky confided, the darkness and the moonlight giving her a newborn confidence to speak her innermost thoughts.

"You're right, it is incredible to look at," J.C. said, standing close by her, "but I'm not sure about it being the heart of this place."

"You don't think so?" She took a step or two around the edge, her feet just inches from the water. "It probably sounds silly to you."

"No, not at all. I just think the heart of this place is the people here. The water draws the people, but it's folks like you, Becky who really care. That's the true heart of the spring."

She was glad he couldn't see her blush despite the moonlight. "You are more than kind, J.C. Thank you. I don't mean to sound ungrateful, but I'd best say good night here and not have you coming any closer to our house in the dark. Homer will start barking and Pa can get pretty itchy with a shotgun after dark."

J.C. was not certain if she was serious or teasing about the shotgun part, but he decided not to find out. He took both her hands and looked at her, without speaking, for a long moment.

"Good night then, Miss Becky Darling. It has been a truly wonderful evening, one I'll never forget." With that, he turned and walked back the way they had come.

Homer padded out to greet Becky silently as she approached the darkened house. She sat down on the porch steps and scratched his ears for him. "You doing a good job of keeping an eye on things here?" she asked him as the big dog leaned happily against her. "Oh, Homer, I wish you could give me some advice," she half-whispered to her companion.

They sat in silence for only a moment before Becky heard a cough in the darkness and Homer's explosive bark launched him from the porch. "Homer! Homer!" Becky tried to call him back, but to no avail. "Who's out there!?" she demanded of the darkness.

"Becky! Becky!" The harsh whisper was choked in hoarse laughter and a scrambling noise out of sight in the darkened woods.

"Who is it?" she called again.

"Becky, it's just me. Homer, come here, will ya? Shut up, boy! It's just me, Jake!"

"Oh, heavenly days!" She stepped off the porch as Jake and Buster Kendrix tumbled out of the dark shadows. "What are you two idiots—"

"Who's out there?" Becky heard the creak of the door and the pumping action of her father's shotgun behind her.

"Pa, it's just me!" Becky cried out. "Just me and Homer, not to worry!" She grabbed hold of her brother and pulled him down low to the ground.

"Becky, you entertaining folks at this late hour?" Her father's voice sounded calmer than his first shout but still heavy with concern.

"No, Pa, it's all right, honest. I'll be in directly. I promise." She heard the door close and she breathed a sigh of relief.

"What are you doing out here?" She turned back to her brother who was lying on the ground, with Homer standing over him. He and Buster were weak with laughter.

"Oh my stars! You're drunk!" She straightened up in disgust. "You're lucky Pa didn't shoot you both!"

"It ain't all our fault, Becky." Jake managed to pull himself to his knees, while fighting off the dog that was now intent on welcoming him with a dog-delivered bath. "Stop, stop, Homer." He fell over again, laughing. "Our car run off the road and we come to borry Pa's mules to get her back on the road and then we can—"

"You come to get Tick and Tock in the middle of the night? You are crazy with 'shine! You'd be lucky if'n Pa would let you have them when you're stone cold sober in the broad daylight, Jake! He ain't about to let you near 'em at this time of the night!" She spit out the words between clenched teeth and hoped her father didn't guess who was out here in the woods at this hour.

"How we gonna get our car out without 'em?" Jake began to whine.

"Listen to me!" Becky grabbed hold of her brother's shoulder and squeezed hard. "How far is your car?"

"Just a little piece down that way." Jake tried to point in the direction he wanted but couldn't manage to do so in his disoriented state.

"Good," she stated in a matter-of-fact tone. "You go back to it and sleep in it 'til daylight. Maybe by then, you'll have some sense about you. You come back after sunup and talk to Pa then. He ain't going to do anything with those mules at this hour and you certainly aren't going to get anywhere near 'em, do you hear me?"

"You don't have to go getting so bossy, little sister," Jake's companion spoke up for the first time. "We just wanna borry 'em for a little while—"

"I don't care what you want, Buster!" Becky turned her fury on him. "You get near my house or barn and I swear I'll call my Pa and that'll be the end of that! Do you hear me? The only reason you two aren't full of double-ought buckshot right now is 'cause I was out here. Now get on back to your car and sober up!"

The two stumbled off in the same direction from whence they'd come.

Becky stood silently in the moonlight until she could no longer hear their crashing clumsy footsteps. Homer returned to her side, tail wagging, and looked up at her as if to ask what was next.

"Come on, Homer," she called as she walked back to the porch.

"Becky, who was that?" She heard her father's voice call out softly as she slipped inside.

"It was Jake, Pa." She sighed as she leaned against the door for a moment. "He said his car slid off the road and he thought you might be able to get him out with the mules. I told him to go sleep in his car 'til morning and then come back then."

She heard an undetermined sound from her parents' bedroom and then she realized her father was trying to muffle his own laughter. "Good girl," he finally managed to say to her. "You and Homer make a good team."

Chapter 8

She couldn't read her father's demeanor the next morning when he came in for his usual hot biscuits and coffee. He didn't have much to say to her, simply ate and picked up Benji to take him to school.

"Is he all right?" Becky asked her mother after the two of them had left. She set the now empty coffee cup and biscuit plate in the metal sink. "I guess Jake didn't come back this morning."

"No," her mother answered with a sigh, as she stood kneading dough to make bread. "Never heard another word from him. Why didn't you bring him in last night? He could have slept on the floor at least or---"

"Ma," Becky interrupted. "He wasn't alone. He was with Buster Kendrix and they were both drunk." Becky looked down at the floor and wondered if she should have withheld the truth, but she was tired of covering for her brother.

"Oh."

"Is Pa all right?" Becky changed the subject. "What does he say now?" She picked up a rag, dampened it and wiped off the couple of dozen eggs that she'd collected in her basket yesterday from "the girls," as her mother referred to their chickens.

"He was still unhappy when we came home last night," Hannah admitted. "That's why I told him I was pretty tired and didn't care to stop at the inn. I hope you didn't mind too much."

"Well, I missed you. That's for certain," Becky answered honestly. "I wish you could have been there, Ma. Everyone was so happy, no arguing, no carrying on like they all have been for weeks now. It was such a relief. Red Flaherty even fetched his fiddle and played for everyone when Miz Josie asked. It was a nice change, like a real party."

"It sounds like it was a good time." Her mother frowned as she stopped to add flour to the table where the dough was trying to stick. "Your father was still cross, hurt mostly, I think. He's simply convinced that this park thing is not going to bring all the advantages that the politician is promising, but it's really just one man's opinion against another's right now. Your father came home talking about how it's not his place, if the neighbors are all convinced that they want it, to stand against them. Like everyone else, we are just going to have to wait and see. And that's hard but it's especially difficult for your father."

"He's not always so patient." Becky nodded in agreement.

"A trait he's passed along to his only daughter," Hannah added, casting a sidelong glance at Becky.

"Yes, I guess that's true." Becky giggled. "I've got to go, Ma. Oh, I almost forgot. Miz Josie said she'd like some cabbages to make cole slaw if we have any."

"Well, of course, there's always cabbages at this time of year." Her mother smiled. "Get a gunny sack and take half a dozen to her this morning from the garden. Tell her to pay whatever she thinks is fair when she pays you for the milk later. The dear woman pays ten cents a gallon for milk so I'm sure she'll pay what's right for the cabbages as well."

"Thanks, Ma." Becky skipped out the door.

The big garden that lay to the east of their house was always a delight by early summer. All the hoeing, weeding and planting was starting to pay off in a big way. Becky loved summer more than any other season, despite the Ozark heat and humidity. She knew part of it had to do with the variety of good things coming out of the garden all summer long.

Cabbages, lettuce and spinach were actually past their full bloom, and she and Benji were scrambling to get them cut, used or sold before they went bad. Meanwhile, so many other green plants, sweet corn, tomatoes, peppers, squash, beans, cucumbers, pumpkin, okra, turnips, and potatoes, were all up and growing strong with the promise of much bounty to come. And then there were the strawberries. She could eat them until she was fit to burst. She snagged a couple of the first ripened berries, wiped them off on her skirt and bit off their tops, enjoying the sweet tartness while she gathered her cabbages.

At the inn, she discovered she was still tired from the night before but she didn't let it hinder her efforts. She had things to get done, especially as the week drew to a close. There would be more guests tomorrow, so she had things to prepare in advance. She could work tomorrow, if needed, although Miz Josie was usually kind enough to give her Saturday afternoon off if she could manage it. One thing was for sure, she didn't work on Sunday. Her father had been adamant about that when she took this job. Tourists or no tourists, her father forewarned her, there would be no working on the Sabbath and Josie Bennett Smith had agreed to that upon hiring her.

The day sped by like so many others, and she was surprised when, at the end of the day, she saw Jake outside the inn. He was still in the rebuilt touring car, talking with J.C. Shine of all people.

"Hello there." She spoke to them both as she strolled up. J.C. stood next to Jake's car door, earnestly discussing something, and jumped perceptibly when she approached.

"Hello yourself." He recovered quickly.

"And where were you earlier last night?" Becky asked her brother pointedly. "Buster said you were busy and then you show up---"

"Aw Becky," he interrupted her as he reached out and jerked on a piece of her hair. "You know I ain't got no interest in that politicking and park talk," Jake drawled. "So how was it anyway?"

"You two know each other? Of course." J.C. corrected himself immediately. "I forget this is a smaller community.

"Small community, huh?" Jake snorted. "I don't know about that, but yeah, you could say we know each other. This is my kid sister."

"Oh really? I had no idea." Genuine surprise played across his face and yet at the same time, Becky noticed his countenance relaxed as if a weight had been lifted from his shoulders.

She couldn't get a read on what they had been discussing before she approached, but she decided to let that go and turned instead to answer Jake's question. "Last night was really a good time once they got the meeting over down at the confluence. Miz Josie invited everyone back here and made quite a celebration out of it. Too bad you weren't here. It was more party than politics by the time the evening was over."

"That's true, it really was." J.C. agreed. "It was nice to meet you, Jake. Jake Darling then, I assume."

"That's me." Her brother grinned. "Hey, got to get going, Sis."

"So how did you get your car out of the ditch last night?" Becky finally cut to the real question on her mind.

"Oh," Jake snickered. "Once we woke up this morning, we found it wasn't that hard, with me driving and Buster pushing. We managed."

"So I see." Her attitude remained decidedly cool.

"Good to see you, kiddo. No time to be giving rides home today. Buster's a-waiting on me." He gunned the engine of the Ford that was still running as rough as the last time she had seen him. The engine coughed but didn't die as he shoved it into gear and took off up the hill, away from the inn and the town of Brice.

"Rides home?" J.C. looked at her with a question on his face.

"Oh, he came by once and gave me a ride home in that car." Becky watched him go with a frown on her face and a worry in the back of her mind. "Right after he borried it the first time from Buster. I wish he would come home or at least quit working for Buster Kendrix."

"Really? And Buster is...."

"A no good moon—." She cut herself off in mid-description. "A no good monster of a man who runs a no account saw mill up on Poker Ridge. He was at the meeting last night. Maybe you saw him. Tall, ugly bean pole who wasn't wearing nothing but a pair of overalls and a hat."

"Oh yes, I did see him." J.C. nodded. "Quite the local character, I gather."

"Hmph!" Becky snorted. "That's the polite way to put it, I suppose."

"Not one of your favorites, I take it." J.C. noted her reaction with amusement.

"You take it right. He's one of those people who just reaches out and takes others in, do you know what I mean? He don't pay the boys who work for him hardly nothing and it's a slipshod operation. That's how Pa puts it. Likely to cheat you as not and I don't like to see my brother tangled up with that sort."

"I don't blame you. Why does your brother stay there as opposed to somewhere else?"

Becky shook her head and turned along the road to begin her walk home. "I don't know, because those boys up on the hill are known for being the party kind, I guess. Living up there, answering to no one, working when they want to, drinking and…well, you get the idea."

"I see," J.C. said nothing more.

"So you going to be here through the weekend, I take it?"

"Yes, it looks that way." J.C. fell into step beside her. "I think the senator had hoped to wrap this up sooner but now, after the meeting last night, we have appointments scheduled through much of the first of the week. I don't think that he really planned to do that many individual interviews, but after the offer he made last night in front of everyone, he can't very well go back on it."

"No, I guess he can't," Becky giggled. "Kinda got caught in his own net, didn't he?"

"Pardon me?"

"Well, he went fishing for a few and caught so many, now he's caught in his own net and has to stay longer than he first thought."

"Yes, that appears to be true." J.C. smiled. "Not that I'm complaining, mind you.

"No?"

"Oh, no! What a wonderful place to work! Nothing wrong with this at all." He spread his arms wide as if to embrace the entire valley.

Becky thought he looked more handsome even than that first day she had seen him. Today he wore a seersucker suit with tiny stripes that made it look to be a soft blue at first glance, but no tie. The suit brought out the bright blue of his eyes, she thought.

"So, you going to walk me all the way home again?" She stopped to look out at the water and realized she was already halfway there.

"Do you mind?" he asked, carefully gauging her response.

"No." She laughed softly. "I don't mind, although I can't say my pa will feel the same."

"Maybe I should come all the way to your house this time and ask him, and make certain he knows I'm not saying or doing anything he would find objectionable."

"Well, that would seem like a good idea." Becky thought as she spoke. He certainly has the right instincts. "But I'm not sure it would go down too well with him right now."

"Why?" J.C. inquired. "You're not promised to someone else or anything like that, are you?"

"Oh, my, no." She laughed at the thought. "No, it has more to do with the fact that you work for the senator and why you're here. Right now I think my pa still sees you and the senator as the enemy, kind of like the scouts for an invading army if you will."

"Oh, I never thought of that. That means you must be providing aid and comfort to the enemy with working at Miz Josie's hotel and visiting with us."

She giggled as he continued the metaphor. "Well, yes I suppose so. I just think he needs a little more time to adjust to the whole idea of it. A park, I mean."

"I see. Well, will you do me a favor then?"

"If I can," she answered honestly, watching his face closely.

"Will you tell me the minute you think it's safe? I would very much like to talk to him, and make certain he's not upset with me for visiting with his daughter."

"I'll keep an eye on things." Becky gulped and tried to keep her voice even as she answered, while studying her shoes. "If and when I think he's feeling better about things, I'll be certain to let you know."

"Good." He nodded in agreement. "I'd appreciate that."

* * * * * *

Sunday morning found Becky eagerly looking forward to church. She had forgotten until her mother said something last night that today was Baptism Sunday. Seven individuals were set to be baptized this morning after worship and her mother was up earlier than usual, making sandwiches on home-baked bread, slicing up yellow cake that she baked the night before, serving up strawberry marmalade to be drizzled over the cake. She added a salad made from fresh poke and dandelion greens, and a half gallon of buttermilk. With so much food to be taken down the road, along with their own serving plates and such, Pa brought the wagon around for Hannah and Becky. Benji rode in the back with all the picnic items. Zeb had his prize team of mules, Tick and Tock, hitched to the wagon and, as always, he rode his mustang, Betsy, alongside.

The white clapboard church was packed to overflowing this morning, due to the summer season and the baptism. They usually scheduled the main baptisms of the year on

Easter Sunday, but this year, Easter had dawned as a day of rain and flash floods. Things weren't much better the Sunday after, so those in charge had postponed that part of the annual celebration a few more weeks and combined it with a 'dinner on the grounds', as the locals often referred to a picnic after worship held on the church property.

Becky was surprised to see J.C. and the senator standing outside the church door as they arrived.

"Good morning." J.C.'s jovial greeting welcomed them all to their own church as if they were the visitors rather than the other way around.

"Good morning yourself," Becky answered back.

"Good morning, J.C." Becky was pleased to see her father shake hands with J.C. as they went into church.

"May I sit with you?" J.C. asked. "The senator felt it would be proper for us to join people here in worship this morning and I agree. He's off talking with some others so if you don't mind…"

"You are welcome to join us." Her mother spoke up first. "Glad you wanted to come." J.C. slid into the last pew next to Becky and her little brother.

Becky found the enthusiasm of the morning message combined with the elation of sitting next to J.C. an extraordinarily exhilarating experience. She could never have imagined feeling so free of spirit as she did that morning. It was as if she woke up to this first day of the rest of her life, the way she wanted the rest of her life to be forever. She tried hard to concentrate on Rev. Louie Bennett's words that morning, a near impossibility. She loved Louie Bennett, as did all of the local parishioners, the rare woman preacher in these Ozark hills. She had come to Bennett Spring many years before with her father, George Bolds, a tent revival preacher. Louie Bolds had married William Sherman Bennett, Miz Josie's brother and the owner of the majority of the acreage the state now wished to purchase for their first park. Along with others, they had built the little church in the valley not so many years ago.

"It is when we stand in the wilderness that we are most likely to hear God's voice." The preacher's voice echoed throughout the little church. "When God directed Moses to lead the Israelites out into the desert, He knew that would be the place they would be able to hear God's voice better than any other. Without the distractions of the Egyptian rulers, ordering them about, demanding bricks to be made and so on. Out in the desert, He would perform miracles for them, from water from a rock to manna from heaven, all so that they would know He was their God and that He loved them. So when we are discouraged, feeling as if we are truly lost, we need to remember, God is never lost to us. When we are in the wilderness, that is where we are most likely to hear God's own voice."

Becky stole a glimpse of the man at her side as the congregation bowed their heads for the final prayer. Her heart leapt at the sight of his eyes closed in reverence and she was thunderstruck by the realization that, for the first time in her life, she was falling in love.

She was more than familiar with the attraction between boys and girls, young men and women. For the last year, Jake had delighted in teasing her about how much Cletus Meyers was in love with her. She was fond of Cletus, too, but as a sweet boy she'd known since they were younger than Benji, nothing more. Others her age had gotten married in recent years and her friend, Georgia, was in love with every new boy she met, but this was something new and different for her. She couldn't help but wonder, too, what it meant that the first time she could truly identify the sentiment, she was sitting in God's own house of worship.

Chapter 9

People were on their feet, talking, visiting, making their way out the door, heading down to the river at Louie Bennett's invitation. Her father, the Rev. George Bolds would be baptizing the folks who were 'giving over their lives' for the sake of the Gospel this morning.

"They are baptizing people this morning?" J.C. spoke softly in her ear, tickling the nape of her neck with his soft breath and sending a thrill down her spine.

"Yes," she managed to find her voice. "Do you want to come?"

"Well, I don't know." He hesitated.

"Good morning, children." Josie's voice echoed across the church. "Good to see you here, J.C. Come on! We're going to see a few of these folks get dunked and then we have a huge spread to set out for everyone."

"Oh, I don't mind to come along, but of course, I didn't bring anything for the dinner."

"Hmph! None of these men did!" Josie chortled. "You'll fit right in. We've got enough food lined out here to feed a small army, so you better come along or we're going to have a lot of it going to waste and there's absolutely no point in that. There's nothing to eat at the inn today because it's all out here, so come along with you now."

"Yes, ma'am," J.C. laughed as all of his excuses were tossed aside.

Despite her father's frown which she caught sight of from time to time, Becky stayed close to J.C. and told him who each person was as they were baptized, from 8 year old Greta Brown to 67 year old Mortimer Stillingham, who held out for years, despite his wife's pleadings. Earlier in the year, he'd been caught out in an open field in a thunderstorm and nearly been struck by lightning. After that, he couldn't get to church fast enough and today, he was making it official.

The new converts came out of the spring water, shivering but happy with smiles on their faces, and were greeted by a jubilant congregation. Afterwards, folks gathered back near the church. The food was bunched on tables beside the church and after filling their plates, some found a seat on benches, rocks or stumps. The majority spread out on blankets and quilts to enjoy their meal.

Josie had spread an extra large quilt next to Becky's family's quilt. "Have a seat," she told J.C., saving him the embarrassment of looking for his own place to sit. "Can't have you standing over there like some waif with no place to go now that you got your plate full."

He grinned his appreciation as he settled down on a corner, next to Becky who sat near him, but definitively on her mother's own homemade quilt. Becky recognized Miz Josie's quilt as having come from one of the upstairs rooms at the inn.

"What a great day!" Josie Smith spoke to anyone within earshot. "The weather is perfect, so much better than trying to do this at Easter. I realize that be the Lord's most special Sunday and all, but the weather in this part of the world is so often dreadful like as not. I wonder if the weather isn't better in Palestine around Easter time?"

"Now that's a thought I must say that never occurred to me," Hannah chuckled as she scooped up a bite of Trudy Stone's turtle stew.

"Wonderful stew, Trudy." Hannah reached out and patted the hand of the woman who had cooked it as she walked by.

"Well, thank you, Hannah." Gertrude Stone stopped momentarily to share a word of conversation. "That's no small praise coming from one of the best cooks in the valley."

"You are most kind, Trudy," Becky's mother answered. "You know your own way around a kitchen quite well, I daresay, and this stew proves it."

"It is so very tasty." Josie Smith chimed in.

"Hmm." Trudy Stone cast a critical eye in Josie's direction by way of acknowledgement but said nothing more as she moved away to her own place.

Becky watched as J.C.'s eyes seemed glued to the receding figure of Mrs. Stone, but he said nothing as he busied himself over his dinner plate.

"Hey Zeb!" Someone called out to Becky's father once most had finished their meal. "Tell us the history of Bennett Spring."

"Yes, Zeb, recite it for us, please." Others joined in the call.

Zebulon Darling blushed slightly and shook his head. "Go on, Zeb," Hannah muttered and gave him a push on his shoulder. "They love to hear it the way you tell it."

He traded glances with her and then slowly put his plate down and climbed to his feet amidst sporadic applause and the occasional whistle.

"He's going to do it!" Becky whispered excitedly to J.C. "Listen to this!" Her eyes shown with anticipation as she set down her plate and turned her full attention towards her father.

Zeb walked over and retrieved a pair of metal spoons from the table, carefully wiped them clean and then settled himself on a tree stump that one of the other diners quickly vacated. He tested the spoons, clacking them together and putting them to his ear, as if testing their tone, making sure they were just right. His audience laughed appreciatively at his antics.

Then he began in earnest clicking the spoons rapidly in time to his chanting.

"In 1837, James Brice and his wife Ann

They came from Illinois and they had a little plan

To travel far and wide, in search 'twas such a fling,

And they settled in this lovely place that we call Bennett Spring.

They had two girls with them,

Daughters, Anna and Jane

And the next thing you know

They're all grown and anything but plain.

Jane soon married Asahel and Anna went to John,

Then came Nancy Jane, Anna Caroline, and our own Uncle Jim."

Zeb interrupted himself and pointed at an older man with a white beard and longer hair who stood at the edge of the crowd, leaning on a walking stick. Uncle Jim Clanton, as he was known throughout the valley, raised his hand and waved and the whole crowd cheered, and then called for more, at which point Zeb continued.

"Life is sad at times, John passed and Anna wed another

Peter Bennett Junior, another mill man now, came to be her lover.

And today, their children are here with us, William Sherman and Miz Josie."

Another round of applause followed as they were acknowledged with whistles and cat calls of approval. Zeb continued his recitation, spoons ever clacking.

"Then there's lots of others down the line,

Gladys, Bertha, Francis David and Arlie

Again the crowd acknowledged a younger man off to one side with their applause, who waved and laughed as Zeb included Arlie Bramwell in his chanting poem.

Then other families called this valley home,

Their names too numerous to mention,

Ruth and Smith and Hawk and Conn,

It sounds like a convention!

There's Browns and Mullicaines, Andersens, and Darlings too,

These lines were, of course, followed by a great big grin as he stopped long enough to point to Hannah and himself, mugging for the crowd, and then he slowed to a stop as his epic poem drew to a close.

And as history goes, ol' Bennett Spring flows,

For that, my friends is all that be

For home folks, travelers, fishermen three

For scribes and singers and knaves like me!

Zeb Darling brought the spoons to a halt and stood up to take a bow to the rousing applause and laughter of an appreciative crowd.

"That's quite good." J.C. laughed along with all the rest. "Did he write that?"

"Yes, he did," Becky answered as she continued to clap for her father. He took another couple of bows and then slid back to the ground beside his beloved Hannah.

"Pa loves history," Becky added. "That was his way, he said, to pay his respects to the history that has gone on before us here at Brice. He actually has a much longer version as well that talks all about the Indians who were here before the Brices and the Bennetts."

"That's pretty incredible." J.C. stood up and lent her a hand to do the same. "Do you have time to take a little walk?"

"I think so." Becky looked over at her mother who was leaning up against her husband now that he was settled once again at her side.

"Go ahead." Her mother nodded in her direction. "Just not too far and not too long."

"Yes, ma'am." Becky smiled her gratitude and the two of them walked across the green carpet of grass towards the mill race and the mill, now deserted and quiet on a Sunday afternoon.

As they walked away from the crowd, Becky noticed a different air about him, as if he was troubled in a way she couldn't quite fathom. She watched the thick green grass beneath their feet and turned her steps towards the cedar tree out in the center of the field.

"So what was life like in those faraway places like Panama and Cuba?" she asked, trying to find something that would fill the sudden silence and bring the sunshine back to his eyes.

"Oh, interesting. Very busy, of course, but that's just because in both places, we were in big cities. Lots of hustle and bustle in Panama City and Havana."

"Ah-ba-vah." She tried to imitate the way he pronounced the Cuban capital.

"Oh, sorry." He shrugged with a grin. "That's the way they say it there. You say Havana. They pronounce it differently, with no "H" and the a's sound like 'ah's'."

"I see." She tried again. "Ah-bah-nah."

"That's right." He nodded.

"I went to St. Louis once," she said, as she skirted the large cedar tree out in the middle of the field.

"There you go. Then you know exactly what I mean."

"I do?" She looked up at him.

"Sure. Pretty much a big city is a big city. I mean, the language they speak may vary but in reality, the similarities outweigh the differences, as far as I can tell."

"Really?"

"I think so. What did you think of it, St. Louis?"

"Oh." She laughed lightly, as they walked along the mill race. "I didn't think much of it to be honest. Too many people, so much noise. I went with Pa, just the two of us, to see his father. He was coming to visit us all the way down here. He came on the train from Ohio, but he got sick and they put him in the hospital instead. So we took the train from Lebanon and went to see him. We stayed with someone Pa knew from years ago who lived in a...what did they call it? A flat in St. Louis."

J.C. grinned. "A flat, yes, an apartment in the city."

114

"Yes, all those people jammed in together like that. It was real different, I'll give you that. We walked along in front of some of the big stores in downtown St. Louis and looked in the windows but Pa wasn't much for shopping, especially not worrying about his father and all. The Mississippi River sure was big. I'd never seen that much water before. Makes our little rivers around here look pretty tame." She smiled at him. "Anyway, we visited my grandfather in the hospital and that way I got to meet him. We saw him some the next day and after that we came home. I did like the train ride though. That was real interesting, just watching the world fly by your window."

"Yes, trains are a fine way to travel," he agreed. "So what became of your grandfather?"

"Oh, he got a little better and was able to go back to Ohio. He died the next year, so Pa always says he's glad we went up to St. Louis as that was the last time he ever saw him."

"I imagine so." J.C. remained deep in thought. "So do you have any plans for the future?"

"Well, of course, I do." She looked at him askance, as if he were an idiot. "I intend to marry and settle right here, just like my parents, and raise lots of babies."

"Good for you," he commended her. "There is a great deal to be said for knowing what you want to do and where you want to do it."

"I suppose that's true," she replied. "I can't say I ever thought about it much, but I've always known that's what I wanted. I mean, going on the train was thrilling and I wouldn't mind to do it again and go someplace new, Kansas City or Chicago or even to California. A great many people talk about that place so it must be very interesting, but I can't imagine moving there or living anywhere else. This valley is home. Traveling about is exciting but this is where I would always want to come back to. This is where I live."

"Yes, it is." He eyed her thoughtfully as he spoke. "I can see that, and you really do live here, too."

"What do you mean? Are you making fun of me, J.C. Shine? I know I probably seem like some country bumpkin to you but—"

"No, no, quite the contrary." He hurried on in an attempt to explain himself. "I meant that most sincerely. You do live here in every good sense of the word. You have your work, your friends, your family. You are of service to others. There is nothing wrong with any of that. To be quite honest, I envy you, Becky Darling. You know exactly who you are, where you come from and what you want to do with the rest of your days. That is no small feat in this world, I assure you."

"Oh." She squirmed at the unexpected compliment. "I just thought…"

"I think it is a wonderful life you live here and…" His voice trailed off. His gaze drifted to the road as an open Model A passed by. Jonathan and Trudy Stone were on their way home from the church dinner.

"Who is she?" Becky put her concern into words. "Who is Mrs. Trudy Stone to you? Ever since you saw her the other night, you cannot keep your eyes from her. She is old enough to be—"

"Trudy Stone. Yes, well, I'm not sure, but I think…" He reached into his inside jacket pocket and drew out a slim leather wallet. He pulled out a tin type photograph and handed it to Becky as they arrived at the mill. She leaned up against the large wooden front porch of the mill.

"Why do you have a picture of Mrs. Stone?" she asked as she closely studied the image of a younger but truly beautiful woman.

"That isn't her," he answered.

"It's not?" Becky looked up at him in confusion. "But it looks exactly like her, only younger and prettier."

"That's a photograph of Fiona McGillicuddy Carter Shine. My mother." He looked out at the swift moving water beyond them.

"McGillicuddy? That was Mrs. Stone's name when she came into the valley. Ma still calls her Trudy McGillicuddy Stone sometimes when she's aggravated with her. Does that mean...?" She gasped at the realization. "She's your mama's sister?"

He put his foot up on the concrete footing that ran alongside the mill and leaned against it, his arm resting on his knee, and looked back out across the water.

"It would seem most likely." He swallowed hard before speaking again. "I would say that yes, she is my mother's sister, her only blood relative, except for me. That would also make her my aunt."

"Oh my goodness sakes, J.C!" Becky reached out and took his arm in her enthusiasm. "And you had no idea that she was here? And your mother, she doesn't know either, does she? So your mother, she was on the orphan train, too, just like Mrs. Stone. Ma told me about them the other day when I asked her—" she caught herself in mid-sentence.

"Well, never mind what I asked her," she rattled on breathlessly. "The important part is she told me how Trudy McGillicuddy first came to this valley and she said before that she'd come from New York on an orphan train. Do you know about those trains?"

"Oh yes." He chuckled as he looked down at his shoe and rubbed aimlessly at a scuff mark there. "My mother told me all about life on the streets of New York before they came west and about the train itself and the stops along the way." He sighed and looked over at his companion.

"But this is so exciting, J.C!" Becky could hardly contain herself. "We've got to go talk to Mrs. Stone. She's your aunt, for heaven's sakes, and we've got to tell her."

"No." He said in a quiet yet adamant tone. It was so unlike her father, whose opinion could be heard some distance away when he was trying to make his point. This man, whose demeanor was calm and controlled yet so gentle, was no less resolute.

"It's not our story. It's theirs." A sad little smile slipped across his face. "I can't go barreling in, no holds barred, not knowing all the details."

"I don't understand." Becky's head wagged slowly back and forth.

"It's a matter of respect." J.C. straightened up. "It will have to wait. As soon as I get home, back up to Holt's Summit, I'll tell my mother about seeing her and how much she looks like her. Then it will be her choice as to what to do about it."

"What to do about it? What do you mean?"

"Just what I said." He smiled patiently at her enthusiasm. "This isn't about my life or yours. It's about theirs and they should choose whether it gets upended, digging up a great many memories that may or may not be happy ones."

"Oh." Becky handed him back the photo and all but collapsed against the side of the mill building. "I never thought of it like that."

"I know," he said, as he tucked the photo inside the wallet and the wallet back into his pocket. "I probably wouldn't have either except that, like I said, my mother talked to me about it when I was growing up. Actually, she was telling me how wonderful it is to have a family, and how she and her sister, Trudy, had started out life without one. Their mother died young and their father was always in a bar somewhere, drunk. They landed first in an orphanage and then on the train. My mother said her sister was the one always taking care of her, defending her because my mother wasn't very big." He laughed. "She still isn't for that matter, although there's enough fire there, ounce for ounce, to get anything accomplished that she wants done!"

He continued with his story. "Her sister was adopted out first. The couple who took her off the train wouldn't take my mother because she was so little--underfed, I suspect-- and perhaps they thought she was sickly as well. At any rate, the two sisters were split up and it was heart-breaking to both of them at the time. A few stops further down the line, my mother was adopted by a wonderful family named Carter. She still talks lovingly about how good they were to her for the years that she was with them."

"The years that she was with them? What happened?"

"Yes, that's part of the tragedy of it all. They died when my mother was still in her teens, during a cholera epidemic. My mother got sick too, but she came through it, but both her adoptive parents died. Later, when she met my father, Joseph Shine and his three boys, she said she discovered a whole new family and it was like being adopted all over again."

"Three boys? You said you had brothers but..."

"They are actually my half-brothers, Joseph, James, and Josiah. Their mother died when Josiah was born. My mother went to work for them as a governess, to take care of the boys when Josiah was nearly five and Joseph and James, the twins, were seven. That's how my parents met, so all my brothers are several years older than me, just as my father was ten years older than my mother. The Shine family took her in so completely that my dad used to joke that if he and my mother were ever to go their separate ways that he feared his parents would keep her and throw him out!"

Becky laughed as the more jovial side of the man she had come to know over the past few days returned.

"At any rate, she has talked often of how important it is to have family, in good times and bad. My father died last year, but my mother still lives with his parents, her in-laws, and I'm sure always will. They depend on her now as much as she depends on them. I can't upset that balance without her permission. I will certainly tell her about finding Mrs. Stone and that she is here. If she wants, I will bring her myself to meet her but it must be her choice. You see that, don't you?"

Becky nodded silently and much to her surprise, her eyes were filled with tears.

"I think my mother has had a good life," he added, deep in thought. "Despite a truly rough beginning, I think she would tell you the same thing. She is a happy person, so if she were to decide that she doesn't want to stir up painful memories from long ago, that should be her choice as well."

Becky cleared her throat. "You are absolutely right," she replied in a soft voice. "I won't say a word to anyone, I promise."

"Thank you, Becky. I so appreciate that."

His eyes met hers with a smile and her heart took wing. His mother must be so proud, was all she could think.

"Come on, I want a closer look at those little trout up there in the fish hatchery. Can you show me?"

"Sure." She smiled and scrambled after him. "Arlie Bramwell runs it and he'll show us all around."

Chapter 10

The new Reliable butter churn worked amazingly well and Becky was quite pleased with it. Even Benji had less to complain about as he helped her make the butter. He liked sitting on the floor, wearing short pants and wrapping his bare legs around the jar while he turned the crank. He said it kept him cooler that way churning butter on a hot day. She also noticed that, like her, he enjoyed peering through the sides of the glass jar to actually see the butter as it formed. She wished she could think of a way to tell Mr. Taylor away off in St. Louis how much she appreciated it, but she decided she would simply have to wait until the next time he came back to Bennett Spring.

At the inn, J.C. and the senator were busy all day long with their interviews, but she had plenty of work to do as well. Farmers were starting to come along on a regular basis now with their wheat ready for grinding and, that was one more question the senator had to answer often. What would be the fate of the mill if the state bought the area for a park? As she'd understood what she heard, the mill owners had a ninety-nine year lease with William Sherman Bennett. She couldn't help but wonder how that might complicate things. Still, the question at the moment that tugged hardest at her heart was how much longer before J.C. would be returning with the senator to Jefferson City. That was a painful thought she managed to keep pushing aside every time it crept in, while she was washing dishes and changing bed sheets.

She saw him at noon each day and served dinner to him, the senator and many others, farmers, locals, and even a couple of area businessmen who drove out from Lebanon to continue to encourage the senator to give the area a favorable report in Jefferson City upon his return.

The week had come too quickly to an end as far as Becky was concerned, and she knew the time was near when J.C. and the senator would be climbing back into their fancy touring car and heading north.

"Becky." Her head snapped up from the dishes she was washing as she heard her name in a half-whisper, coming from near the back kitchen door of the inn. She dried her hands on her apron as she walked to the back. J.C. was standing outside, his hat in his hands, and she stopped in the doorway at the sight of him.

"Becky, things are moving pretty fast now and the senator is making plans for us to return to Jefferson City. I wanted a chance to talk to you before we go." He coughed slightly, more nervous than she had ever seen him. "I'm sorry. I didn't want it to be like this, catching you at your work and all, but it's been so busy and I certainly didn't want to go without, without…" He looked down at the ground and then straight up at her, "Without telling you how I really feel about things."

Becky stepped outside and closed the screen door behind her. "It may be sometime before I can get back here. But I wanted to say, I want to come back, if that's acceptable to you. I'd like to write to you too in the meantime, if you have no objection. I mean—"

He was interrupted by a boy on a large bay horse as he galloped in from the Wire Road side of the valley. "I got a telegram for the senator!" Little Larry Meyers, Cletus's younger cousin, who wasn't much older than Benji, reined his horse to a stop in front of the Brice Inn as he shouted. "Senator Wiggins. I got a telegram for—"

"Here, boy." J.C. stepped out from the back of the inn and waved a hand. "I'm the senator's aide and I'll see that he gets it." He handed the boy a quarter.

"Wow, thanks Mister!" Larry was loudly appreciative of the tip.

J.C. caught the look of surprise on Becky's face and grinned with a shrug. "It's a long ride from town and the senator will pay me back."

Becky smiled and wished he could return to the back door and pick up where he had left off, but she realized that probably was not going to happen.

"I'll be back," he told her as he headed inside to find the senator.

Becky returned to her dishes, pondering each and every word that J.C. had said earlier. Calm down, she told herself as her heart began to catch up to her racing thoughts. All he really said was that he wanted to come back to Bennett Spring, and doesn't everybody who leaves here say that, one way or another, before they go? He also said he'd like to write to her, she remembered. The truth is she had been caught so off-guard finding him out in the back like that, she couldn't remember exactly what he said.

A few moments later, she heard footsteps hurriedly pounding down the stairs. She found J.C. in the parlor speaking to Miz Josie. He gave her a big wink as he climbed the stairs again, two at a time.

"Well, there's a surprise," Josie said as she walked over to her. "The senator had said they'd be leaving tomorrow, Saturday morning, but now J.C. came down to say they are staying over."

"They are?"

"Seems the senator just got a telegram from another one of the senators there in the capital and they are coming on

Monday. They requested that the senator wait for them to join him here on Monday, so it looks like our guests will be here a few more days."

"That's not a bad thing, is it?" Becky tried to keep the excitement out of her voice, but it was apparently a failed effort as her boss gave her a long sideways look.

"I'm sure some folks think so," Josie quipped off with a grin. "Gives you and J.C. another couple of days to get to know each other. Not a bad thing at all."

"Miz Josie." Becky blushed and turned back towards the kitchen to finish the dishes.

Surprisingly, J.C. did not come back down from the upstairs room and Becky certainly couldn't go up to talk to him, much as she would have liked to. She dawdled in the kitchen for as long as she dared and came out to the parlor table to find Miz Josie doing accounts. It would be another hour before anyone came in looking for an evening meal, and she knew she should start towards home since there were chores always waiting there. Still, she had hoped she might hear a little more of what J.C. had on his mind. Apparently, however, it was not to be.

Out on the front porch, she hesitated a few more moments and walked down to the gate, rather than climb over the fence as she did most days. She saw Benji running down in front of the Bennett Store with a group of boys about his age and then remembered it was Friday, when the Boy Scouts met. He had recently joined the pack, that's what they called themselves, and from all that he said at home, he was enjoying it immensely. Becky turned her steps towards home, but she didn't get far before she heard a vehicle speeding up fast behind her. As fast as it was moving along the gravel road, she turned and stepped aside expecting to see her brother Jake or some other reckless young man his age go speeding by. Instead, she was surprised to see Deputy

Cletus Meyers come to a sliding halt on the gravel, where he was quickly surrounded by a cloud of dust.

"Becky!" He called out as he jumped from the vehicle with the gold star on its side. "You don't know where Jake is, do ya?"

"No, Cletus, I don't," she answered as he ran up to her.

"Da—" he checked himself. "Dang it! I was really hoping against hope, he might—"

"Cletus! What is it? What's wrong?" She followed him back towards his car and the color drained from her face.

He slouched into the drivers' seat. "Buster Kendrix is dead."

"What? How? What happened?"

"You know what he's been doing up there on the hill, don'tcha?" He surprised her with the question.

"Well," she hedged. "I know what I think he's been up to. That's all. It's not like I've been up there in a long time."

"You know Buster was making 'shine, moonshine, and that Jake's been in it with him. I suspected as much the day I stopped you, but I didn't have no proof and I didn't figure you were in it with 'em. 'Course I could have been wrong…."

"Cletus, I love my brother but you know I would never be mixed up in—"

"I know, Becky." He held up both hands. "I didn't think so but I had to be sure."

"So what happened to Buster and what's this got to do with Jake?"

He heaved a sigh. "Buster got himself shot, by none other than Lenny Franks. They were in it together for awhile, making more and more. It looks like Lenny was their front man and did such a good job of selling they couldn't keep up. They started taking short cuts, or I should say, Buster did. Seems he didn't tell Lenny everything he put in there and when Lenny found out, he shot him."

"Oh my heavens, Cletus!" Becky shook her head as she folded her arms tightly across her middle. "And my brother?"

"Well, I'm looking for him, Becky. We got Lenny and he said Jake wasn't there when the shooting broke out."

"Shooting?"

"Oh, yeah." He pulled off his hat and wiped his brow on his shirt sleeve and replaced his hat. "Buster didn't go down easy. He shot Lenny too before it was all over. It's a wonder those two fools didn't put a bullet in their own still and blow up the whole hillside." He snorted in disgust. "The worry now is where Jake is and if he's out delivering bad 'shine. If somebody drinks that stuff and dies or gets all crippled up, well....Jake's in it up to his neck, Becky. I'm sorry to be the one to tell you."

"It's all right." Becky patted Cletus's arm as it rested on the open window of his vehicle. "I'm glad it was you and not somebody else who didn't care. I've got to go tell my parents, although heaven knows I'd rather not!" She turned away from him.

"You want me to come with you?"

"No." She shook her head. "I appreciate the offer but I'll do this. It'll be bad enough, just me by myself. They always wanted so much for Jake to do good and he just don't seem to know how."

"I know what you mean, Becky. I've already found that out in this kind of work. I see it all the time. Good folks mixed up in bad company."

She nodded as Cletus started up his vehicle and drove away towards Lebanon in search of her brother.

Becky walked on, part of her wanting to hurry to the safe haven that home and family offered in times of trouble, and part of her wanting to put off the delivery of such devastating news. She hadn't gone far when she remembered the last time she had seen Jake. He'd seemed more jovial than ever, talking with…talking with J.C. Her heart skipped a beat as she whirled, doing an about face and headed back towards the inn.

She glanced upstairs as she approached the building. She didn't want to talk to anyone except J.C. Perhaps her suspicions were unfounded. She certainly hoped so, but these days you could never know for sure. More than a few good people that she knew openly defied the Prohibition Laws of the day and purchased illegal liquor, some more discreetly than others. J.C. and the senator were from the big city, the capital of the state. It would not surprise her if…

Raised voices from the back of the inn where the senator's car had been parked for days now drew her attention. She slipped around the side of the building and saw the senator seated on the edge of the open trunk of his fine car. He was talking, no, practically shouting, at J.C. who was standing over him. The vehemence of the senator's argument surprised her and drew her back into the shadow of the building.

"I can't believe the audacity of that son of a buck, Senator Jack Harvey." Clarence Wiggins fumed from his perch. "He ordered me to stay here, to spend another weekend in this Hillbilly Hades to wait on his arrival on Monday. We should have been done with this days ago. Harvey isn't looking for anything except a free trip to go fishing at the taxpayers' expense." He snorted and reached into the trunk. He pulled out a tall bottle of clear liquid and took a long swig before setting the bottle back out of sight.

"You sure you don't want some?" the senator slurred to his aide. "It does help to make this place more bearable."

"I don't find the need, Senator, I assure you." J.C.'s voice was low, an example he seemed to be trying to set for the senator but with no luck.

"I tell you this whole venture has been a fool's errand if you ask me. This is not the kind of place where the state needs to spend money luring in tourists. By glory, people don't want to come sit in the woods for days at a time. The city is where they'll want to flock to if they've got the time and the inclination. They need a place where there is actually something to do and something to see. Fine restaurants, theatres, moving pictures, some real entertainment for pity's sake, which is readily available in St. Louis. They held the World's Fair there twenty years ago already. It's a place of sophistication and civilization. Out here, there's nothing but fishing and---" He stopped to slap at his neck. "Mosquitoes, ticks and hillbillies." He sat staring at the palms of his hands as if he expected to see at least one of the three materialize right before his eyes.

"Senator, please." J.C. turned towards his boss. "Let's go back upstairs. Surely with some rest, you'll feel better and then—"

"No need, my boy! No need!" The senator waved him away. "Who was that preacher who used to live around here? He wrote that book, what was his name? Wright, that's it. He wrote that novel that got everybody all excited about Branson a few years ago, what was it? The book about the shepherd."

"*The Shepherd of the Hills.*" J.C.'s voice cut through Senator Wiggins' ranting once again "Harold Bell Wright wrote it."

"That's it. I knew it was something about a shepherd. He got everybody all wound up about this part of the country but it won't last. You mark my words. People will lose interest in that place pretty quick once they figure out these hills are full of nothing but mosquitoes, ticks and hillbillies." ·

He snorted and started to laugh. "That's it. Mosquitoes, ticks and hillbillies, maybe I should write a book. I swear if I have to talk to one more ignorant hillbilly about anything I may well lose my mind. All we've got out here is one bunch that doesn't want anything to change ever and the other bunch wanting to take the state's money and get every bit of it they can!" He gestured wildly, nearly losing his balance and falling off the end of his vehicle. He reached inside the trunk once again for the bottle and had it halfway to his lips when Becky stepped out of the shadows.

"So is that what you really think?" Becky ignored the drunken senator and directed her fiery question at J.C. as she came forward.

"No," he said. "No! Becky I'm so sorry you heard that, but please know..."

"What I know---" She waved him away as he came towards her, his arms outstretched as if he might embrace her, if she would only allow it. She gulped as her emotions welled up in her throat, threatening to cut off her words. "What I know is that I came back here to warn you. To find out if possibly—" Her gaze fell in disgust on the disheveled senator. "Where did you get that?!" she demanded suddenly and reached for the bottle in the trunk.

"I beg your pardon!" The senator tried to stand but found that his knees would not cooperate and propel his rotund body in the direction he wanted to go. Instead, he swiped at Becky as she snatched the bottle, an action that very nearly landed him inside his own trunk.

"Becky, what is it? What are you doing?" J.C. was now truly alarmed.

129

"Just answer me!" she demanded again as she turned back on J.C. "Where did you get this? Answer me that and this hillbilly's daughter won't bother you anymore!"

"I...I," he stammered and looked at the grass beneath his feet. "I arranged it with your brother, Jake. I didn't actually purchase it from him. I told the senator when he asked that I wouldn't do that, but I did set it up so that the senator himself could—"

She whirled and threw the bottle against a large rock that sat alongside the road, sending glass shards flying. "Why did you do that?!" Now she was the one raising her voice. "Don't you know anything about moonshiners and their nonsense?" The sobs she had managed to stifle ever since Cletus told her could be held back no more. "It ain't always safe! Drinking that stuff could cost you everything! The law's out looking for Jake right now because of a bad batch of moonshine that's already got one of his partners killed!" She was screaming now but she didn't care. None of it mattered anymore.

"I didn't like it, believe me!" The shocked senatorial aide managed to find his voice and make his plea. "I actually felt better about it once I found out he was your brother. Maybe that sounds foolish now, but at the time---"

The owner of the Brice Inn appeared at the back door. "What in the name of the saints and the sinners is going on out here? Becky, what's wrong? Senator, are you feeling all right?" Josie looked from one to another but got no answers.

"You're right!" Becky glanced over her shoulder. She felt even worse at the sight of Miz Josie, but she couldn't stop now. "It was a foolish thing---" She turned back on J.C. "But then, he's just a dumb hillbilly. What did you expect? That's all there is here. Isn't that what your boss said? Well, I've done my part! I've done my best to save his sorry soul from poisoning by bad 'shine and that's all I aim to do!"

"Becky, please." J.C. stepped close to her and wrapped a strong yet still gentle hand around her upper arm. "Let me talk to you." His intensity was almost frightening, but her fury wouldn't let her stop.

"About what?! Mosquitoes, ticks and hillbillies! I don't think I ever want to talk to you again, J.C. Shine!" She pulled her arm away and ran towards the open road that led towards home.

Chapter 11

When she woke up the next morning, her head was pounding so hard she had to shield her eyes from the sunlight pouring into her upstairs loft bedroom to blot out the pain. She had always loved her room, tucked up under the eaves of the house her father built. Her brothers had shared the space across the way, the two rooms separated by a heavy curtain. Until just a few months ago, Jake as well as Benji had slept over there. Now Jake was gone and all her fears of recent weeks had come to pass. He was never coming back.

When she came in the house the night before, her face streaked with tears, her mother had simply asked, "J.C?"

Becky managed to nod her head but she couldn't bring herself to say anything more.

Her mother asked a couple of additional questions, assuring herself that the man had not hurt her physically or done anything untoward.

"No." Becky had managed to choke out the words. "He didn't hurt me like that, Ma. He didn't do anything like what you're saying. It was my fault. I believed…" She hiccupped and tried again. "I believed in him more than I should have, is all."

"Oh, Becky." Her mother wrapped loving arms around her sobbing daughter. "That's what we do as women in this world and we get our hearts broken every time, I'm afraid. I'm so sorry. Is there anything I can do?"

Becky shook her head. "I just want to go to bed, Ma. Can I do that, please? I know it's early but..."

"Go on with you." Her mother released her and gave her a little push towards the ladder to the loft. "I'll tell your father you're feeling poorly and I sent you to bed. That's certainly not a lie in and of itself. Get some rest. You've been working so hard, at the inn and here. Being fatigued makes a broken heart feel even worse. Tomorrow things will look better. I promise."

She cried all night, long silent sobs that shook her whole body but with no sound. She couldn't have her father or Benji wondering what was wrong with her. Tears soaked her feather pillow long before she finally cried herself to sleep. Now in the morning light, however, she discovered her mother was wrong. She had finally slept but nothing was any better and she knew she couldn't put off the inevitable any longer. She had to tell her parents about Jake and the encounter with Cletus yesterday. If she didn't, it was a surety that someone else would. She opened her eyes again. She could feel how puffy they were, sore and red. She got dressed, albeit slowly, before climbing back down the ladder.

She still had to go to work this morning, although she was obviously going to be late. Her mother was downstairs and Benji was, as always, right there, underfoot.

"Benji," Hannah spoke up as fast as her daughter's feet hit the floor. "Take the egg basket and go check the girls, will you? I got busy yesterday and didn't get the chance to do it."

"Oh, Ma." Benji started to complain.

"Benji." His mother's correction was surprisingly mild, Becky thought to herself. "What is that they're teaching you down there with the Boy Scouts? To do your duty to God and your family and others? Isn't that your promise?"

"Yes ma'am," Benji answered politely.

"And didn't your pa and I have a talk with you about the extra help that was going to be needed around here in the months to come? That starts now, young man, and that means, no sass."

"Yes ma'am." Benji retrieved the empty basket and headed out the door.

"Thanks, Ma." Becky made it across the kitchen and reached for a coffee cup. She didn't usually care that much for coffee but today it was the only thing that sounded good. She wondered idly if the senator had as big a headache as she did this morning.

"How are you?" A worried frown crossed her mother's brow as she asked the question.

"Oh, Ma, everything is just awful!" Becky dropped herself into a kitchen chair, the coffee sitting untouched in front of her.

"Becky, honey, I know it might seem that way right now, but..." She hesitated, not sure what to say next.

Becky grappled with her thoughts, trying to think where to begin. "Where's Pa?" was all she could think to say. If she had to tell them the truth about Jake, she wanted them to be together, partly for their sakes, partly for hers. She didn't know if she had the strength to tell the story more than once.

"It's Saturday. He's working, of course, but he should be along any time now."

The door opened as her father whisked inside. One look at his face and Becky knew she was too late.

"Buster Kendrix is dead," were the first words out of his mouth.

"What?" Her mother's head snapped up.

"Buster Kendrix is dead," her father repeated, "and the law is out looking for Jake."

"Oh, heavenly days!" Her mother closed her eyes tightly and was immediately in silent prayer.

"Oh Pa, I'm so sorry." Becky's tears returned with a vengeance, making her head hurt all the more.

"You knew about this already?"

"I heard about it yesterday afternoon, it's true. Cletus stopped by the inn and told me. There wasn't nothing to be done about it, truth be told. At least, this way you and Ma got one more full night's worth of sleep before you found out." She dropped her face in her hands, elbows resting on the table, as Benji came through the door with a full basket of eggs.

"Look at all I got!" He announced proudly but no one answered him.

"What's wrong with Becky?" he asked innocently. "Pa?"

"Benji." His father reached out and grabbed him up in a bear hug. "Come on, I've got to find my own biscuits and coffee this morning. Give me a hand, will you?"

Zeb looked over at his wife still seated in the corner, who said nothing but simply returned her attention to the loom, which he noticed she was working with increased vigor. "Well," he commented to no one in particular, "I guess I don't have to wonder any more about why you kept tossing and turning last night." He reached out and rubbed the back of Becky's neck. "I don't know what to say, girl. I really don't. I wished you'd have been the one to tell us, but I understand, for what it's worth."

"Oh, Pa, I wish I had too!" Becky's tears overwhelmed her once again. She stood up and Zeb wrapped his arms around her as she cried on his shoulder.

"I've got to go, Pa." She stood up straight and attempted to pull herself together. "I'm so late now Miz Josie probably thinks I'm never coming back. I'm sorry I didn't get to the milking this morning and—"

"It's already been taken care of. You don't hear no cows out there bellerin', do you? You weren't even stirring by that hour this morning so I didn't think you'd be up for it. I got to it, although I don't mind saying, I do hope you don't make a habit of it."

"No, sir." She managed a weak smile in spite of her tears. "I won't. Thank you for taking care of Maggie and Marge this morning. I'll see to it that you won't have to do it again."

"I understand." Her father patted her back. "Your ma told me about that senator's aide, too, about him not being all you had hoped he would be. I was afraid of that. Just don't worry about them flatlanders, you hear? We don't need them and they don't need us and that's just the way it was meant to be."

"Oh, Pa." She shook her head. She stood on tiptoe and kissed him on the cheek. "See you later." She scooted across the room and hugged her still silent mother, but noticed the mute tear running down her cheek.

"Oh, Ma," was all she said. She turned quickly to go as her father walked over to the loom and took his wife in his arms, pulling her away from the weaving.

"Let's take a short walk," she heard him say as she closed the door. They would get through this together. She wished she had someone to lean on as well.

She dreaded the thought of having to see J.C. again. She tried to think of how she might avoid him, but she could see no way of doing so without having to explain her situation to Miz Josie and she certainly didn't want to do that.

The many charms of the exquisite emerald woods that surrounded her on her walk were lost on her this morning. Even the little mink that always made her laugh saw her pass this morning without so much as a glimpse of acknowledgement.

She slipped inside the front door of the inn, wondering what she might do first so that she wouldn't have to speak to anyone. Out of habit she checked the register first and there was a double entry under the 'Checked Out' column, Sen. Clarence Wiggins/J.C. Shine, Saturday.

She ran back out the front door and around the corner of the building. Indeed, the fancy touring car that so many had stopped to admire in recent days was no longer parked behind the building where it was when she left late yesterday. She slowly retraced her steps.

What was that oft repeated phrase of her mother's? "Be careful what you pray for." Had she not just thought how much she dreaded seeing J.C. again? Now that she no longer had to cross that bridge she felt even worse. Oh, why did it all have to fall apart in this way? She didn't even know who to blame. Her brother? The senator? J.C.? Herself? She leaned heavily against the end of the building and let her tears fall freely.

* * * * * *

The summer days were coming to an end, and the nip of fall could be felt in the dawn and dusky evenings of late September. The breeze warned of the coming of colder days and nights, despite the bright days of golden sun. Becky thought about the frosty mornings that would soon envelope the entire valley. All the trees along the stream bank would be dipped in white as steam from the cold spring waters that would still be warm compared to the frigid air temperatures would trim anything near the stream in delicate frozen lace.

Despite the farmers who were lined up now at the mill to get their wheat ground, Miz Josie would be closing the inn in another month once they were gone. Taking her annual vacation is what she liked to call it. The cold weather would keep tourists and farmers all tucked warm in their own homes and leave the inn vacant. Becky would be without a job and the valley would be considerably quieter. Pretty as the snow and ice could be at times, she had really come to hate winter. At least visitors, with all their comings and goings, helped to keep her hands and mind busy, even as her heart continued to ache.

Jake was sitting in the county jail and had been for nearly three months now. Three of the men who'd drank the tainted liquor he delivered had become desperately ill and one had very nearly died. She sat in court with her stone-faced parents as they listened to the judge sentence her brother to a year in the county jail. Her heart had broken, for Jake and for her mother and father. She had never seen them look so hurt, so helpless, and the truth is, it had rattled her faith right down to its roots.

Her new baby sister, Esther Mae, was nearly a month old and she was a delight. Ma had named her Esther, she said, because it was a name meant for one who might do great things and one day save her people. Perhaps that would be this baby's destiny. She couldn't imagine.

Becky loved holding her, watching her every expression, waking or sleeping, while she tried to decide if she looked more like Ma with her haunting dark eyes and curly hair, or more like Pa with his sandy colored hair and light gray eyes. Esther's eyes were a deep blue and her wisps of hair were dark blond swirls, so it was hard to tell who she really favored.

Becky had been at her mother's side when baby Esther arrived in the world. Miz Darcey Mims, the local midwife, had come and she had let Becky help. She told Becky she was a natural and asked if she would like to learn more. Miz Darcey said she needed a helper and she was ready to teach someone else how to help the women of this area when their babies came. Despite her personal sadness, Becky had agreed. She loved her new baby sister, and helping others to add that kind of sweetness to their life was the only antidote she'd found that seemed to ease the pain in her heart, even a little.

Like everyone else, Miz Josie adored Becky's new baby sister. All the talk of the state park had died away for the most part, and when Becky asked one day, the hotel owner told her she thought the whole thing had now passed.

"That Senator Wiggins, he turned out to be a real piece of work. You heard about him, didn't you?"

Becky shook her head.

"Well, never mind." Josie shifted gears. "Now Senator Jack Harley, who came along the week after Clarence Wiggins was gone, was a real negotiator and a much better businessman, but even he couldn't put all the pieces together." She let out a sigh. "I don't expect to see nothing more come of it. I guess it was just never meant to be."

It had taken a little time before Becky realized that only she and J.C. had witnessed Senator Wiggins's rant that last afternoon. She had never breathed a word of it to anyone. How could she? How could she explain how much his words hurt? And then what was she to say? That the senator, despite all his fine oratory to the contrary, had clay feet and that along with his charming aide, had left town without another word? What did that make her except a foolish little country girl who had believed every word "the flatlanders" had told her? Much as she hated to admit it, it looked like her father had been right all along.

Even so, Becky still thought about J.C. every day, especially each day at the inn. Some little part of her wanted to believe she would come into the parlor and find him waiting for dinner or see him outside, ready to go fly fishing in his high boots and funny cloth hat.

She had prayed hard that J.C. was all right and that he might even come back like he'd mentioned that afternoon at the back door. But the truth was he hadn't even written to her like he'd also talked about that day. In her heart of hearts, she knew chances were she would never see him again.

Still, in those times of prayer, she had felt some relief. There were no lightning bolts, no great revelations, only a vague sense of peace, as if God was hovering nearby, waiting. And in a real sense that is how she felt so much of the time, as if she were waiting, but waiting for what? For her life to take another unexpected turn? No, she decided, she was waiting for her heart to start again, to care again. These last few months, except for the new joy that Esther had brought to them, it felt as if her heart had quit working altogether.

"Becky," Josie commented one day right after the noon meal when they had fewer guests than usual. "You look as pathetic as I feel today."

"Ma'am?" Becky looked up from where she had been poking at the fresh apple cobbler that Josie had baked earlier that morning. It was one of her favorites but her appetite had also been on the wane of late.

"You just look, I don't know..." Josie leaned back in her chair and peered at her. "Down in the mouth, as the boys used to say, or maybe you're just tired. That new baby keeping you up nights at your house?"

"No ma'am." Becky looked down, feeling the color rise in her cheeks. Please don't guess, please don't guess what's really wrong, Becky prayed.

"I think you need some sunshine. That's for sure," Josie announced. "Leave them dishes for a bit and go take yourself a walk out there before you start back to work."

"Ma'am?" Becky was confused.

"You heard me," Josie fussed. "I'm tired of this place, too, I swear, and you make me even more tired to look at you, nothing personal, mind you. If'n I could find somebody to buy this place today, I'm a-tellin' you, it'd be gone."

"Miz Josie!" Becky was caught totally by surprise.

"Why so shocked?" Josie looked up as she moved dishes out of the way and picked up her accounting ledger.

"I wouldn't have minded selling this place to the state for a park, I don't mind telling you, but now, I just might look for someone else. Surely there's somebody out there who might like to run their own little hotel. I've enjoyed it the last few years but I'm tired, Becky. I'm ready to move to town and go to work for somebody else, clerking at a store maybe, all day during the week, half a day on Saturday, and call it good."

Becky was pensive as she wandered out the front door and walked along the road, meandering towards the spring branch. Brightly beckoning sassafras leaves added a splash of color to the early autumn green, and acorns would start to fall soon. It would be time to collect black walnuts before long and she'd seen persimmons already hanging in the tree branches.

She stopped to watch a fisherman cast out a long line from his fly rod. Again and again, she watched, staring, as the line flowed far out in front of him and then whipped back over his head as he flipped it behind him to make the return trip. The elegant splendor of his graceful movements in the dazzling afternoon's rays mesmerized her as golden sun rays framed his every movement. She couldn't help but remember an afternoon earlier in the summer spent watching another graceful young fisherman cast a line upon the waters of Bennett Spring.

After several minutes, the fisherman moved downstream and Becky walked back up to the road. An older car, a two-seater Hupmobile, pulled to a stop alongside the road a few yards past her. Another graceful fisherman stepped from the driver's side of the car as a red-headed woman climbed out of the passenger seat.

"Oh, son," the woman exclaimed, with the faint hint of an Irish lilt to her words. "It feels so good to stop and stretch. What a beautiful place this is! 'Tis truly just as you described."

"Becky?" The driver called out to her and waved with a tentative smile on his face.

If her feet had not been rooted to the soil, she might have turned and run. Instead, it took all of her strength to control her quaking knees and make some semblance of a polite reply to J.C. Shine and his companion.

Chapter 12

"**B**ecky, it's so good to see you!" His exuberance caught her as much by surprise as his unexpected appearance. "Come, I want you to meet my mother." He introduced her.

"This is Fiona Shine. I've been telling her all about this place, practically since the day I left here." He laughed easily as if there had never been a cross word between them.

"Mrs. Shine." Becky held out her hand in a polite gesture and shook the hand of the beautiful woman whose sepia-tinted photo she had studied on a Sunday afternoon. Why did it seem like that was so very long ago, Becky wondered.

"Becky, I couldn't wait to get back here." J.C. pulled himself up straight and took a deep breath as if the air in the valley was extra invigorating. "After I told Mother all about Bennett Spring and the town here and....well, it took a bit before I could get things squared up and buy a car, but she wanted to come too and....You seem surprised to see us? Were you not expecting..." His voice trailed off.

"No, I am surprised." Becky grappled to pull her scrambled thoughts together. "It's quite all right, really. Your mother will want to freshen up and wash the dust off after your long drive, I imagine. Miz Josie is over at the inn and I'll be right there."

"All right." J.C. made an effort to check his obvious enthusiasm. "We'll meet you over there then. You're coming now, right?"

"Yes," Becky answered, without drawing any closer. "Right away. You go ahead."

They climbed back into the roadster and puttered on down the road.

Becky's head and heart were both reeling as she walked unsteadily towards the inn, her feet raising tiny dust clouds with each step as she followed the vehicle.

"Heavenly days, will you look at her?!" Josie didn't hide her shock upon meeting Fiona Shine. "She's the spittin' imagine of Gertrude Stone! How is that possible?" She was still exclaiming when Becky came in the front door of the inn.

J.C. dropped a pair of bags on the floor beside the registration desk as the proprietress gave him the keys to the two best rooms, both upstairs. "I'd like to take just a few moments, Jerry." His mother turned to him. "Then I'll be ready for you to take me to see Trudy, if that's all right. You said you know where her home is, did you not?"

"Yes, ma'am." J.C. answered obediently. "We can do that."

"You want to go with us?" J.C. asked Becky, once again catching her off guard.

"Well, I really should get back to work," she hedged.

"Nonsense!" Josie countered her excuse. "You best be going along if you're invited. It's not every day one comes across this sort of thing. It all looks pretty exciting to me!'

A wide smile broke across Fiona Shine's face and Becky could not only see J.C.'s expression in hers, but she also caught a glimpse of what Trudy Stone might look like if she smiled more and fussed less.

"Mrs. Stone lives with her husband near the saw mill and your car has only two seats." Becky tried again.

"Matters not." J.C.'s mother spoke her mind without hesitation. "You're a lovely slim girl. We'll both fit in that seat, with a bit o' squeezin', if you don't mind. And if we don't, we'll make Jerry walk. Do you know how to drive one of these contraptions?" she asked Becky directly.

"No, no I don't," Becky admitted with a laugh. She already liked Mrs. Shine a great deal.

"Me neither. I guess we'll have to keep him," she shared in a conspiratorial whisper. "We'll just make him move over a wee bit if we need more room. Please say you'll come with us. I know it would mean so much to J—"

"Yes, well, Mother." J.C. interrupted as he kept his eyes on her. "If she doesn't feel—"

Suddenly she found her voice. "I'll come," she heard herself say, and in the time it took to move their baggage upstairs, she found herself on the porch with J.C. waiting on Fiona.

"So you told your mother all about Mrs. Stone, just like you said you would." Becky broke the awkward silence between them.

"Yes, and I told her she could write to her here care of Brice, Missouri, but she decided not to do that."

"Why?"

"Hmm, well, I'm not sure. She said as she remembered her sister, this way would be better. She said she would be able to tell immediately by her reaction whether it was a good thing or a bad thing to find her. She said if it's not so good, then she would understand and just walk away and that would be that."

Walk away and that would be that. Becky wondered why she couldn't be that clear cut about things in her own life.

"She called you Jerry." Becky said it as a statement, rather than the question she intended.

"Short for Jeremiah. Jeremiah Carter. She doesn't care for J.C. Says its *sounds* like a politician, whatever that means."

"Jeremiah Carter." Becky rolled over the name she had never before associated with him. "You said your brothers were Joseph, James and Josiah, all Biblical."

"Oh, yes, that would be my father's doing. And my mother's, too." He smiled. "Just like yours, if I'm not mistaken."

"Yes." Becky grinned in spite of her discomfiture.

"My mother used to tell me not to complain about my name. She said she loved the idea of naming me Sonny or Sunny Shine but of course, Father wouldn't allow that."

"Oh my." Becky said. "I have a new baby sister, Esther."

"You do? Esther, now that's a fine name, too. Must be pretty exciting, having a new baby in the house."

"Yes, it is." She nodded without saying anything more.

Fiona Shine joined them on the front porch, and a few moments later the two women were tightly ensconced in the front passenger seat of J.C.'s small roadster, amongst giggles from all of them. Becky eyed her seat companion and thought she seemed to be the kind of person who could make any venture into great fun. She couldn't help but wonder what she must have been like in places like Panama and Cuba.

J.C. pulled the roadster to a stop in front of a few tall sycamores near the spring branch, not far from the wood frame house just up the road from the saw mill. They tumbled out and were part way up the path leading to the front porch when the door opened and Gertrude Stone stepped out, drying her hands on her apron.

"If you're lost," she began, "the saw mill is over there and Mr. Stone is—" She stopped speaking as she squinted at the three of them. "Becky Darling, who would that be with you there?" She pulled herself up straight and let out a scream that Becky thought Miz Josie herself must have heard a half-mile away.

"Fiona! Glory be to God! Fiona! Is it really you?!" She clapped her arms so tightly around Fiona Shine, Becky was afraid the younger woman might not be able to continue breathing. The two women dissolved into tears and shrieks of laughter.

"Come in! Come in!" Mrs. Stone tried to herd everyone into her home at once.

"You two, go ahead." J.C. tipped his flat page boy cap towards the two women. "I daresay you have a few things to catch up on. We'll be along in a few minutes."

"Fine, fine." Mrs. Stone's face was now redder than the red streaks that still remained in her mostly gray hair but she was alive in a way that Becky could never have imagined. Her crabapple countenance had melted in an instant into something almost unrecognizable, but beautifully so.

J.C. stepped off the porch and looked over towards the saw mill.

"You didn't get my letters, did you?"

"Letters?"

"I wrote to you, Becky," he said over his shoulder, not daring to look at her directly.

"I didn't receive any letters," she stated flatly.

"I suspected as much just now as I thought about it after the way you looked when we found you on the road," he continued. "But I promise you, Becky Darling, I did write, twice a week, every week ever since I left here three months ago. I wrote over a week ago to tell you we were coming." A sardonic little laugh escaped him. "I even asked you to reserve rooms for us at the inn with Miz Josie."

"Oh my!" Becky drew in a sharp breath. "Oh, I promised myself," she muttered as she took a few steps back towards the car and bit her lip.

"What's this?" J.C. circled in front of her as she reached the sheltering sycamores.

"Oh, I promised I'd not cry another tear over you!" The words burst out and her hands flew to her face.

His arms encircled her and she laid her face against his chest and let her tears fall.

"I certainly never meant to cause this." J.C. spoke softly as the storm passed and he gave her a little hug. "Are you all right?"

"Yes, just a big baby is all." Becky sniffed and he handed her his handkerchief.

"Oh, I don't know about that." He watched the sun dance across the water behind her as he spoke. "I felt like crying myself a time or two these last few months, when I would write and get no response. All I could think was that you didn't want anything to do with me...and that, well..." He took a deep breath. "That was just about the worst thing I could imagine!"

"Oh J.C., it was nothing like that. I promise you!" She stood up straight, her mind in a whirl.

"Are you all right?" he asked.

"Yes." She sniffed as she pulled herself together. "J.C., do you mind terribly? I know your mother just found her sister and all, but I really do need to go check on one thing and then…"

"I think I understand." He gave her a knowing look. "And I think my mother and her sister are going to be fine where they are. Let me make certain and then I'd be happy to take you wherever you'd like to go."

They traveled back down the road, now just two in the car, to the Brice Post Office, housed in the Bennett's Store. "Do you mind to wait here for me?" she asked as he pulled up in front of the building.

"No, I'll be right here," he assured her.

Becky stepped briskly into the store, all business on her mind. Once inside, she nodded to William Sherman Bennett and asked to speak to her father, whom she could see sorting mail in the back.

"Pa." Becky kept her eyes on the front counter as she made her demand. "Pa, I came for my letters."

"Becky? What are you talk—?" Zebulon Darling's eyes settled briefly on his daughter and then drifted past her to the vehicle with the young blond man seated behind the wheel that could be seen out the front window.

"Now, Becky." His voice took on a decidedly different tone. "You know—"

"I don't want to discuss it, Pa, not now, not never. I just want my letters, like any other normal person on your postal route, if you don't mind."

Zeb cleared his throat and looked down. He cast a sideways glance at Sherman Bennett who looked briefly at the two of them but said nothing. Zeb stepped to the back of the room and reached up high on the top shelf and pulled down a small leather pouch. He reached inside and pulled out a bundle tied with twine and carried them back to the front counter.

"Becky, I…" He tried again.

"Don't say nothing!" Becky threatened under her breath. "Just don't say nothing at all. He did exactly what he said he would do. He wrote to me regular and he brought his mother down here to meet her sister. He did what he promised." She turned on her heel and walked out the door.

Back in the car, she let the bundle rest in her lap as J.C. backed the car away and started down the road but toward the spring this time.

"Is there anything I can do?" He finally asked since she had not uttered a sound since they pulled away from the post office.

"How could he…" was all she said, her eyes fastened on the passing scenery. She watched as a ground hog lumbered away from the road and the speeding vehicles passing by, as quickly as his fat unwieldy body would allow.

J.C. guided the car to a quiet place, not far from the spring itself. "Come on," he said, crossing around to her side and offering her his hand. "Let's walk a little."

She accepted his invitation without comment, but kept the letters tucked in the crook of her arm, pressed tightly to her.

"He's a postman, a sworn employee of the United States Post Office. Oh, how often have I heard those words!" Becky shook her head in frustration as they strolled past the oak and hickory trees. "Of all people, he ought to know better."

"Yes, that's true."

J.C. was too agreeable, she thought as she cast a fleeting look in his direction.

"But Becky, he's a father first. And proud as he is to protect the mail and all that goes with it, protecting his daughter, that comes first. If I had a treasure like you, that's exactly what I'd do."

"Oh, J.C., don't start!" She rolled half-filled blue eyes in his direction. "I absolutely don't think I could stand it if you took his side right now." A little sigh escaped her with a shudder.

"Well, whose side can I take?" he asked with a teasing smile. "I have to take the side I understand, and I do understand why he did what he did, even if his stance caused some misunderstanding and some hard feelings on your side…"

"Hard feelings?! You have no idea!" She snorted her response.

"Oh, I think I do," he responded. "You aren't the only one who hasn't heard a word back in three months, remember? I promised my mother I would bring her down here to meet her sister but the truth is I had to come back for myself, to see you and hear it for myself."

"Hear what?"

"Hear you say you wanted nothing more to do with me. After you didn't write back, I decided I'd have to come and see you and hear it directly from you."

"Oh, you did, did you?"

"Yes, I did." He smiled now at the painful memory.

They walked on around the spring, its blue-green waters ever-moving, leisurely making their way to the surface before flowing on.

"And is that what you expected I'd say?"

"Well, I certainly hoped for better than that, but when you don't get an answer for so long…." He gave a little laugh. "It does make you wonder. So, are you going to read those letters, or just carry them around?"

"Oh, I might just carry them around with me for awhile." She sauntered on a step or two ahead of him.

"I see."

"I waited so long, J.C. I was all but convinced..." Sincerity was admirable, she decided, but difficult because of the lump it put in her throat.

"Convinced? Convinced of what?"

"Convinced you were never coming back!" She managed to blurt it all out in one breathy exclamation.

"That's what I was trying to tell you that last afternoon, back by the kitchen door."

"I know. I remember. You have no idea how many times I've thought of that afternoon, but then things went sour with the senator and, oh!" She caught herself. "How is he? You still work for him?"

"Well, no, as a matter of fact, I don't."

"You don't?"

"No, we parted company very shortly after we left here that morning. I found I could not abide the way the good senator operates, to be perfectly honest. It put me in a bind for awhile because I quit before I had another job. Turned out just as well though. Did you know he's up on ethics charges?"

"Oh no! I had no idea."

"Yes, it seems Senator Wiggins holds financial interests with his brother-in-law in property in the St. Louis area, near Forest Park. They were trying to get the state to buy it for some sort of tourism venture."

"Oh, good grief!"

"Exactly. So it was not a bad thing that by the time he was being called upon for answers to those kinds of questions, I had already left his employment."

"I suppose that's true. So what are you doing now?"

"Well, it's been a little of this and that. Helping my grandparents around the farm, making inquiries. Actually what comes next all kind of depends."

"Depends? Depends on what?"

"Hmm. More like depends on who."

She looked up at him and wrinkled her nose.

"I'll be honest with you, Becky. We, my mother and I, came to Lebanon yesterday and spent the night there last night. It was hard not to come the last twelve miles out here, believe me, but I had an interview this morning. As soon as we finished we came this way."

"What sort of an interview?"

"The owner of the *Laclede County Republican* is looking for an assistant editor and a reporter. I talked to him about the position and I promised to let him know by tomorrow."

"So it depends on him?"

"No. He told me the job was mine if I wanted it."

"Really?" She could feel that lump coming back up in her throat.

"Becky." He took her hand and tucked it into the crook of his elbow, as they continued to walk. He smiled as he looked at the letters tucked in her other arm. "Those will tell you, you know?"

"Tell me what?" She looked down at the snug bundle.

"Those will tell you whether or not I want that job Lebanon. I told the newspaper owner I had to make a tri here first." He let out a little sigh. "I left things in an awful lurch when the senator woke me up early that Saturday morning and insisted we drive back to Jefferson City right then, but I couldn't stop thinking about this place and about you, Becky. About the girl who knows just what she wants to do and where, the girl who wants to stay right here and raise babies at Bennett Spring."

She laughed. "Actually, Miz Darcey, the midwife, asked me to help her so now I'm going to deliver babies here."

"So you're getting an early start on things, aren't you?"

She grinned and looked away. He slipped his hand over hers as they strolled on.

"I told the newspaper owner I had to come out and check on something here before I could give him an answer. I had to see you, Becky, and know if I was still welcome."

"Oh, J.C." His name escaped her as a whisper. "You are always welcome here."

"That's all I needed to know." He caught her up lightly in his arms, lifting her feet off the ground as he embraced her. Her arms slid around his neck as his lips found hers for the first time. The precious bundle of letters fell to the ground.

"I think we better go find your mother." She finally spoke after a few moments. "She'll think we've forgotten all about her."

J.C. set her feet back on the ground and grinned. "I suppose you're right."

Becky bent down to retrieve her letters. "I'll not be ___" She gave a silent but heartfelt prayer of ___ nswer to her many prayers these past few ___ glanced once more at the swirling waters

J.C. looked at the car, then turned back to Becky. "Perhaps tomorrow while my mother visits with my Aunt Trudy, you and I could take a ride to Lebanon while I give that newspaper owner an answer about that assistant editor's position?"

The great Bennett Spring, ever true to the beat of life for generations, past and present, continued its languid passage behind them. A sudden breeze swirled green and golden leaves in a tiny whirlwind and scattered them across the sparkling waters in the late afternoon sunlight. The sheltering sycamores stretched their great white arms skyward in an ever-protective arch above the cool blue-green waters. The heart of the spring continued its faithful rhythm as yet another generation prepared to begin its journey in life.

Historically Speaking.......

- Josephine Bennett Smith sold the Brice Inn and its surrounding 8.5 acres on December 27, 1924, to the state of Missouri for the state's first state park, Bennett Spring. Acreage was also purchased that year for Mark Twain State Park. The two together are considered the beginning of the Missouri state park system.

- William Sherman Bennett sold 565 acres to the state in April 1925, which included the spring that still puts out an average of over 100 million gallons of water daily. Four hundred twenty-seven of those acres can be traced directly to James Brice, William Sherman Bennett's grandfather and the original settler in the Bennett Spring area.

- The last of the town of Brice was demolished by the Civilian Conservation Corps (CCC) in the 1930s as part of the establishment of the park. The Bennett Spring Church of God, once a white clapboard building, was covered in stone to more closely match other park buildings in 1954, per current members of the church. It is the only building of the original village of Brice that still exists. Since it is within the confines of a state park, the one acre plot on which the church stands is independent of the park, exempted from state ownership by the contract that was made with the Bennett family. Likewise, the large cedar tree outside the Bennett Spring Park

Store in the 21st century stood in a field out back of the Brice Inn in 1924.

- The Brice Post Office continued to operate until 1965 when the area's postal deliveries were transferred to other post offices in Laclede and Dallas Counties. The postal route that covered Highway 64 west of Lebanon, including Bennett Spring State Park and the entire valley, continued to carry the name Brice Route until the Lebanon Post Office switched over to a route and box system in the late 1980s. That usage was replaced a decade later by the current five-digit address classification that uses road and drive names as part of the 911 emergency system. Dallas County, also covering a portion of the park, established a similar system a few years later.

A Brief History

The first visitors to what we now call Bennett Spring were barefoot and later moccasin-footed. Members of the Osage, the Delaware and Kickapoo tribes were known to have hunted, fished and camped in the area. There is some conviction amongst early historians that the People of the Middle Waters, as the Osage called themselves, did not actually live at or around the spring, but rather simply passed through, believing this to be a sacred area, a place they held in high respect.

They shared a legend that described the original site of the spring as a small pool of great depth. Their best divers could not reach the bottom, despite its calm waters which produced only a small stream of water. Their stories relate that those original native people forgot their traditions, who they were and where they came from. They became proud and arrogant, forgetting their daily prayers and neglecting their responsibilities as stewards of the land that had been entrusted to them by the Sacred One. They killed other Indians and took the scalps of those who were not worthy. One night, after they had returned from yet another shameful raid, the Sacred One's wrath was felt by all as the ground shook, nearby trees tumbled and the earth as they knew it changed forever. The quiet pool became a boiling spring, as ceaseless tears began to flow from the eye of the Sacred One, creating a full and flowing stream that followed along the valley floor all the way to the Niangua River over a mile away. Bennett Spring, the spring we know that produces 100 million gallons of cool fresh water daily, was born.

By the 1830s the U.S. Army had pushed the Indians westward to Oklahoma, leaving behind only thousands of arrowheads, souvenirs left behind by the original inhabitants that decorate the mantels of many local residences and on rare occasion, still delight a sharp-eyed tourist.

In 1837 James Brice, originally from Virginia, and his wife, Ann, of Kentucky, arrived in the valley from Illinois. The forest of oak, hickory, black walnut, elm, maple and dogwood grew dense with underbrush and bears, wolves, panthers, wildcats and even the occasional buffalo were also common. Smaller animals such as raccoons, rabbits, squirrels, deer, fox, beaver, mink, muskrat and wild turkey, most of which can still be seen on occasion, abounded.

In the early 1840s James Brice, then 50 years old, built the first of several mills in the Bennett Spring area. As other settlers moved into the valley, the area became known as Brice Spring. The small village that sprang up on the site of today's Bennett Spring State Park Store was later called Brice, Missouri beginning in the 1860s after the death of James Brice.

Within a few years other settlers and families moved into the valley—Hawk, Brown, Conn, Clanton, Henson, Lomax, Mullicaine and Bennett. Peter M. Bennett constructed a second mill at the confluence, where the spring waters meet the Niangua River, but within a few short years both mills were destroyed by flood waters.

James Brice's daughters, Jane and Anna grew up and married others in the valley; Jane to Asahel Bennett and Anna, per her father's wishes, married John Clanton, a young wagon maker from North Carolina. He and Anna had two children, Nancy Jane and James Madison Clanton, before John Clanton's death in the winter of 1856 at the age of 30. Shortly afterwards in early 1857, Anna Brice Clanton gave birth to her third child, Anna Caroline.

By the 1860s the country as a whole was engaged in the Civil War but the spring area and the tiny town of Brice were protected by their secluded location and lack of a nearby railhead.

The widow Anna Brice Clanton remarried, to Peter M. Bennett Jr. this time. The 427 acres of property, including the spring itself that had once belonged to her father and had been willed by him to her first husband, John Clanton, now reverted fully to her. Upon her marriage to Peter Bennett Jr., all of her property became his and soon the general area became known as Bennett Spring. Peter and Anna Bennett had six children but only two lived to adulthood, William Sherman and Josephine Bennett.

In 1894 the Rev. George Bolds, his wife, Mary, and their four children, the oldest being a 17-year old daughter, Louie Bolds, came to Bennett Spring and held the first of many old time revivals. At their first meeting, 38 men and women were saved and baptized including 29 year old William Sherman Bennett. A year later, he and Louie Bolds were married. In the years to come, Louie and later her son, Paul would become well known ministers throughout the area.

The record is vague as to exactly how many mills were eventually built in the valley. The two original grain mills were both known to have been destroyed by flood and the last mill built by Peter Bennett was constructed close to the village of Brice. It burned in 1895. The last Bennett Spring mill, a grist mill, stood near the location of the previous mill, across the section of land that today holds the concrete hatchery pools built in the 1960s. This mill was a partnership amongst J.H. Hensley, a local cattleman, and Dr. John B. Atchley, Arminta Atchley, John B.'s wife and J. H. Hensley's sister, and Freeman Atchley, a brother-in-law to

Hensley and Arminta Atchley. The new mill partners took out a ninety-nine year lease with W.S. and Louie Bennett for use of the wheel left from the 1895 mill that had burned, the dam floor, water and roadway use rights necessary for the operation of the mill.

The new mill, opened in 1900, once again drew people to Bennett Spring to fish and camp while they waited in line for their wheat to be ground.

Meanwhile, a report in the *Laclede County Sentinel* in January 1900 stated that the Missouri Fish Commissioner deposited 40,000 mountain trout into the spring branch, brought from west of the Continental Divide. While several others, visitors and residents alike, expressed an interest in stocking more trout in the area, an Oklahoma dentist, Charles A. Furrow, and an unnamed business partner were the first to actually invest in the idea by establishing a hatchery at Bennett Spring in July 1923.

Others began to come to Bennett Spring driving Model A's and Model T's or a rented buggy from Lebanon to picnic, visit or even spend a night or two at the Brice Inn, run by Josephine "Josie" Bennett. The residents of the village of Brice, never prosperous by any stretch of the imagination, continued in their daily lives and welcomed the growing number of visitors to their valley.

According to an article that appeared in the December 12, 1924 issue of the *Laclede County Republican*, A.O. Mayfield, the president of the Lebanon Chamber of Commerce, requested that state officials consider Laclede County as a possible site for the first state park.

Soon after negotiations began however, they were publicly called off as the parties involved could not agree. They began again shortly afterwards and on December 27, 1924, Josie Bennett Smith sold the state their first acquisition of land for the new Bennett Spring State Park.

*** Coming in 2011 ***

The Heart of the Spring Lives On
By Laura L. Valenti

A new story of the Darling family and
their lives at Bennett Spring in the 1930s
as the CCC comes to the new park and
shapes the features that have become
famous as Bennett Spring State Park

The Heart of the Spring and soon,

The Heart of the Spring Lives On

Also available at:

www.betweenthestarandthecross.com